"HOW LONG AGO DID YOU MEET?" ASKED A REPORTER.

"Long enough to know that our ultimate goal is totally compatible," Dom said with a straight face.

Well, that was true. They both wanted to go to the Steelers game with enough desperation that they'd walked open-eyed into this ridiculous scheme.

"Give us a kiss," urged one reporter.

"He's too shy," Lynne said.

"He doesn't look so shy to me," the blonde said.

"One little kiss," cajoled the news guy from KDKA.

"Tell them you don't want to do this," Lynne whispered up at Domenic.

"How would I live it down if my buddies see that I passed on the chance to kiss a pretty girl? I think this falls into the area of defending my manhood."

"Make it a good one!" challenged the blonde as Domenic's hands came up to Lynne's shoulders and he spun her around.

He pulled her close.

"Fake it," she whispered.

"What?"

"Just a little peck. Disinterested. So people will know we're doing it because we have to, not because we want to kiss each other."

His lips stroked over hers, so warm and far softer than any man with such hard stomach muscles should have. They were firm, demanding, and she knew that this brief kiss only offered a hint of what Domenic could do with his lips and tongue.

WHAT ARE *LOVESWEPT* ROMANCES?

They are stories of true romance and touching emotion. We believe those two very important ingredients are constants in our highly sensual and very believable stories in the LOVESWEPT *line. Our goal is to give you, the reader, stories of consistently high quality that may sometimes make you laugh, sometimes make you cry, but are always fresh and creative and contain many delightful surprises within their pages.*

Most romance fans read an enormous number of books. Those they truly love, they keep. Others may be traded with friends and soon forgotten. We hope that each LOVESWEPT *romance will be a treasure—a "keeper." We will always try to publish*

LOVE STORIES YOU'LL NEVER FORGET
BY AUTHORS YOU'LL ALWAYS REMEMBER

The Editors

THE WHOLE NINE YARDS

DONNA VALENTINO

BANTAM BOOKS

NEW YORK · TORONTO · LONDON · SYDNEY · AUCKLAND

THE WHOLE NINE YARDS
A Bantam Book / February 1998

ISBN 0-553-44625-8

Published simultaneously in the United States and Canada

Bantam Books are published by Bantam Books, a division of Bantam Doubleday Dell Publishing Group, Inc. Its trademark, consisting of the words "Bantam Books" and the portrayal of a rooster, is Registered in U.S. Patent and Trademark Office and in other countries. Marca Registrada. Bantam Books, 1540 Broadway, New York, New York 10036.

PRINTED IN THE UNITED STATES OF AMERICA

OPM 10 9 8 7 6 5 4 3 2 1

For the real Dominic and Lynn—just
in case you didn't recognize yourselves
because I so sneakily disguised the
spelling of your names

ONE

"Someone ought to invent a way to keep traffic moving when it snows," Lynne complained as she filled her coffee cup. "Then my meeting could have started on time."

"Look on the bright side—you stuck around long enough to get some of this yummy coffee." Beth sipped and closed her eyes in ecstasy. "Ummm. Chocolate-almond with just a touch of coconut. The Steelers won yesterday and are headed for the play-offs. Life is good."

"Life is *great*," said Ellen. "I'm getting married!"

Lynne tapped her coffee cup against Ellen's, just like everyone else. She hopped back laughing, just like everyone else, when coffee sloshed over their hands. But her laugh rang hollow in her ears, coming through a throat that had gone uncomfortably tight, too tight to join in on the congratulations, the demands for details. She kept a bright smile pasted on her face, hoping nobody would notice the envy that gripped her with the remorselessness of a pit bull.

Envious of Ellen? Impossible. Ellen at twenty-five

was only two years younger than Lynne, but stood a good three rungs below her on the corporate ladder. She'd never catch up.

And yet, Ellen's blushing, trembling happiness roused a noxious, twisting curl inside her that could only be jealousy. Heaviness filled Lynne's chest, making it hard to breathe. Absurd. The news probably rocked her so hard because she had always intended to be engaged herself by twenty-five. Engaged by twenty-five, married by twenty-six, a mother at twenty-nine.

But that had been an unrealistic schedule, fashioned when she'd been fresh out of college, before she understood she might not be good enough, smart enough, strong enough to conquer the world quite as quickly as she'd hoped. She'd had to revise her estimates upward once or twice—she hadn't even touched a man, let alone gotten close enough to one to think of marrying him, in ages.

No harm done. She struggled for one even, sustaining breath and then another. She was only twenty-seven. She had plenty of time.

"So Mark finally popped the question." Beth pressed Ellen.

"Not exactly. I told him we apply for our marriage license by four o'clock this afternoon, or it's over between us."

"Brave woman," someone said amidst a chorus of assenting murmurs.

"He can't back out this time," said Ellen. "I have the Steelers on my side."

"What's that supposed to mean?"

"Some guy from the marriage license bureau was on the radio this morning. He's raffling off a pair of Steelers play-off tickets for the couples who apply for marriage licenses today."

Lynne's fingers tightened around the paper cup, crushing it near the bottom the way envy squeezed her chest. Not only was Ellen getting married—she stood a chance of going to the game. Lynne made a big production out of discarding the ruined cup to cover her unwarranted agitation.

"We're boring Lynne."

"No you're not," she protested. "I like men. I believe in marriage. I have both penciled in on my to-do list."

Nobody laughed. Lynne's to-do lists were the stuff of legend around the office.

Susan, Lynne's boss, frowned at her over the top of her mug. "Can you stop by my office before you go downstairs to your meeting?"

"Sure." Lynne feigned nonchalance while her innards started to roil. The group immediately quieted. They all knew, as she did, that OmniCom was set to announce the creation of a new senior management position. They all knew that Lynne had staked all her efforts on earning the promotion. Susan's summons might have something to do with it. Ellen sent Lynne a shaky smile. Beth gave her a furtive thumbs-up.

She ran a quick inventory while she followed Susan. She touched the smooth sweep of her hair to make sure none of the strands had escaped the tasteful silver barrette that held it all back and under control. She ran a finger along her necklace to test that the clasp hadn't worked its way to the front. She brushed at her shoulders and squared them. Let the other middle managers babble about football ticket lotteries and marriage ultimatums—Susan had to have noticed how of them all, only Lynne projected the image of a woman ready to accept the weight of new responsibilities.

Susan gestured toward the chair facing her desk, and Lynne considered how best to lower herself into it. She didn't want to sit too close to the edge—that would make her appear uncertain. Sitting too far back might make her seem overly confident. She settled in the middle, her tension holding her spine rigid, her back ramrod-stiff. Maintaining good posture inspires respect, she'd always heard.

Susan leaned back in her swivel chair and steepled her fingers under her chin. "We decided at the management meeting last night that the new position is a definite go."

Lynne nodded.

"Each department head must submit a list of candidates. The promotion will be awarded after the committee reviews the performance appraisals. I want to make sure you understand the process."

Lynne fought to keep her satisfaction from showing. Even a laid-back company like OmniCom had to pay lip service to procedure. Susan's candor and concern was probably her way of letting Lynne know that this nomination business was nothing more than a formality to allow her to clear her desk before taking on the new job.

That promotion was *hers*—she'd earned it. The past eighteen months of twelve-hour days, the weekends spent working from her briefcase, were about to pay off big, just as she'd planned. All those canceled dates, all the movies she'd missed, all her wistful regrets over friends who'd stopped calling, everything had been worth it. She could almost, *almost*, visualize her parents' proud looks when she told them the news.

"I could wrap up most of my major projects within the month, and—"

"Lynne," Susan interrupted her. "I called you in here because I know how hard you've been bucking for this promotion. I wanted to tell you face-to-face. I won't be recommending you as a candidate."

Lynne blinked while her throat clamped and the leaden weight settled over her chest again. Susan's lips weren't moving, but a mocking chant seemed to reverberate through the room. *You failed. You made mistakes. They'll never be proud of you now.*

She forced herself to breathe. She forced herself to speak.

"I don't understand."

Susan sighed. "A small, innovative communications company like OmniCom needs senior managers who are willing to take risks, willing to use their imaginations. You play it too safe."

Lynne stared in disbelief. Of course she played it safe. Playing it safe, planning and analyzing every step, ensured success. It was one of the unwritten strategies for success that she'd assimilated along with her ambition. "You make mistakes when you take risks."

"Sometimes," Susan admitted. "And sometimes you open a whole new world of possibilities."

Susan leaned forward, earnest and eager as she plunged on, as if she'd been saving all her criticism for this one occasion. "OmniCom wants senior executives to bring fresh ideas to the table. We want well-rounded people with full, rich lives. You never talk anymore about your interests or hobbies. You've grown distant from the other employees. I'm beginning to believe you no longer have a life outside this company, Lynne."

"That's not true," Lynne protested. "I have a life. I have outside interests."

"Such as?"

"Well." She swallowed. Her mind raced, but came up with nothing more than the memories of nights spent slogging through piles of papers, of staring at the screen of her laptop until her eyes burned with fatigue.

"You used to be a real football fan," Susan said. "Remember how we used to tailgate together? And yet you were so quiet out there when we talked about yesterday's big Steelers win that I wondered if you even bothered watching the game."

Lynne hadn't watched. She'd decided at the beginning of the football season that she couldn't afford to spend three hours every week in front of the television set, when it was so much more efficient to listen on the radio and work on reports at the same time. She had trained herself to listen with half an ear, and turned up the volume when the crowd got extra rowdy or the announcer began shrieking in ecstasy. She used to love watching the game unfold in front of her eyes; lately, she'd only relived Steelers triumphs through instant audio replay.

Susan had been right on target—Lynne had always considered her football fanaticism to be her one guilty pleasure. She'd given it up for the sake of this promotion. And now Susan was saying she might have denied herself for nothing. Lynne tamped back a wave of resentment.

"I don't see what football has to do with anything. Unless you're saying it would improve my chances if I roped some poor man into marrying me for the sake of a couple of play-off tickets the way Ellen did."

"No. But it was a gutsy thing for her to do."

Lynne closed her eyes, mentally regrouping. She'd lost her cool there for a moment, lost sight of what was important. That's what happened when she spoke or acted without carefully weighing the consequences. "I wish you'd reconsider, Susan," she said. "I know I'm right for that job."

Susan studied her for a long moment. "I don't have to turn in my recommendation right away. Impress me."

The palm tree's curling bark pressed through the back of Domenic Corso's sweatshirt. He had never leaned against any of the Atrium Garden's botanical wonders—pruned, weeded, transplanted, but never leaned against—until today, when circumstances forced him into unfamiliar, uncomfortable inactivity. He tilted his head back against the trunk and stared up through the tropical foliage to the snow spitting against the glass roof high overhead, willing himself to remain calm until the surrounding uproar subsided.

"Lucky we're not standing in the middle of the lobby, boss." Mike, his assistant, shivered with mock distress. "Those suits'd mow us right down."

"They're rushing to make up for lost time. We had a half-inch of snow over the past hour." Domenic's frustration lent a sarcastic edge to his observation. The minor dusting had ground the morning rush hour to a standstill and sent all the office types into a dither.

The din of pounding feet, dinging elevator bells, and shouted greetings echoed from the marble walls as tardy workers streamed into the Pittsburgh TechnoCenter. Juggling coffee cups and checking their watches, they dashed across the lobby, for once sparing no attention upon the award-winning Atrium Garden.

"Guess none of them'll be standing around watching

us while we work, huh boss?" Mike's disappointment made it clear he didn't mind the bothersome distractions as much as Domenic. "Guess nobody'll be hitting on you for advice."

"Not today," Domenic agreed.

He stared across the lobby to a glass-walled room, willing its door to swing open. The room offered one small avenue of hope, even though it meant exposing his desperation for everyone to see. He hoped it wasn't a bad omen that a lousy, insignificant half-inch of snow had delayed its opening on the only day Domenic ever expected to need it.

"You're really going to do it." Awe mingled with sympathy tinged Mike's voice. "You're going out onto their turf to ask for help."

Mike tended to pepper his conversation with landscaping-oriented phrases. He did it so unconsciously that pointing them out only distracted him and left him blinking with bewilderment.

"I have to try this, Mike."

"There's gotta be something else you can do."

"Anything," Domenic vowed. "You name it and I'll do it, no matter how crazy or bizarre."

But Mike had no suggestions to offer. He glowered unhappily at his toes.

"See? I don't have any choice." Domenic touched the folded note he'd tucked into his front jeans pocket and swallowed hard. It had come down to this: a few words and numbers scrawled across a piece of paper. He'd pursued every other lead. Exhausted every other option.

"I wish I could help you, Dom." Mike clapped him on the shoulder.

"I know. I can't expect you to give up yours."

The Whole Nine Yards

9

"Too bad you don't need a kidney. I have two of those." Mike's crooked smile belied the seriousness of their conversation. "Listen, boss, have you tried Ronny Johnny? He's always bragging he can dig up anything for the right price. I know you wouldn't go within a hundred miles of him under ordinary circumstances—"

"I saw Ronny Johnny yesterday. He can't help me."

Mike's jaw dropped. "You mustn't have offered him enough money. Don't be so cheap, boss. You really rake in the dough, and believe me, sitting around counting it ain't gonna offer you no consolation later."

"I told Ronny Johnny money didn't matter, and he laughed in my face. Said I'd waited too long, it's too late." Domenic tightened his jaw, remembering. Ronny Johnny had widened his gold-toothed smile beyond mere friendliness and commented that Domenic's quandary pointed out the folly of working so hard that he'd lost track of what was really important in life. He hadn't been sympathetic at all when Domenic had pleaded with him to have mercy on a guy who put in twelve-hour days and spent most of his free time helping his family through one crisis or another.

"It's only Monday. You still got almost a week." Mike offered him a weak ray of hope.

"Thanks for reminding me," said Dom.

Only six more days until the AFC Championship play-off game. In this football-mad town caught in the grip of Steelermania, Domenic hadn't been able to pry a ticket out of anyone's hands, at any price.

A few days earlier, he'd resorted to posting notices on bulletin boards. Hell, it had worked for him years back, when he'd been a pimple-faced teenager determined to start his own landscaping business. This time, bulletin boards hadn't produced. He'd hit the supermarkets, the community centers, some of the busier bus stops without rousing so much as a slight possibility. Then he'd remembered the message board hanging in the TechnoCenter's coffee-break room. The tightly locked coffee-break room.

"C'mon," he muttered. "Open the door."

"I never noticed any bulletin board in there," said Mike.

"The attendant always stands right in front of it when she waves to us."

"She waves to us?" Mike craned his head toward the lunchroom.

"Every week for the past three years." Domenic hid a smile. He understood perfectly well why Mike had never noticed the sixty-something lady; with her hair net, squishy-soled shoes, and white uniform, she looked like a nurse or a grandmother, instead of an employee at the ultratrendy TechnoCenter. "She waves so hard that it sets all those little paper scraps flapping behind her."

"Cute?"

"In her own way. I can't picture the two of you together, though."

"I love 'em all, Dom. Just like you."

With an all-male appreciation for quantity over quality, Mike often commented with reverence upon the stream of women passing through Domenic's arms. Mike even claimed to envy Dom's regrets that none of the ladies held his fancy for very long.

As if their conversation had conjured her presence, the break room attendant appeared at the door with a fistful of keys. Sure enough, she waved toward them as she opened the door. The messages fluttered behind her.

"This'll only take a minute," Domenic said, heaving himself away from the palm's trunk.

"Too late," Mike said at the same time.

A horde of suited women surged into the lunchroom. "Did you see that!" Mike marveled. "Looks like they were sucked in by a giant leaf vacuum."

Domenic didn't bother biting back a curse.

"They're planted deep now. Looks like they're settling in for a long, gabby meeting. They all got their briefcases lined up on the table like a row of petunias."

One of the petunia planters began passing out neatly clipped stacks of papers. A few women flipped at once through their copies, exposing pie charts Ross Perot would envy.

Domenic stuck his thumbs into his belt loops and blew an exasperated puff of air toward his forehead.

"Go ahead, Dom, they won't mind you barging in. Maybe one of them'll be so happy to see a regular guy instead of a suit that she'll snatch the note just to get your phone number."

The very thought that his note might be wasted filled Domenic with horror. "Maybe I'd better wait."

Mike dared him. "What's the matter—afraid you'll wilt in front of a roomful of business ladies?"

Domenic couldn't decide whether the reference to wilting was landscaping related or not.

"Are you kidding? I'd *love* walking into that room, even if they all think I'm just another beer-for-brains football junkie in search of a fix. I'll bet every one of them spent at least an hour getting ready for work this morning. They're all perfumed and curled and decked out in hose and heels."

Mike gulped and leaned forward for a closer look.

"I . . . I thought you didn't go for the tough-as-nails business type, boss."

Dom didn't. He preferred the soft, gentle, uncomplicated homebody type. Even so, he held a healthy appreciation for all things female—and it felt nice to pay back Mike for his wilting quip. "I don't have to go for them to like what I see. I'll bet they don't realize how those tailored business outfits just beg a man to use his imagination."

Mike swallowed, hard, and squared his shoulders. "I'll go put up the note for you."

"I'll come back later and do it myself."

"Aw, boss, look at that blonde hogging all the space in front of the board right now. Wouldn't it be, whatchamacallit, ironic if she happened to be the only person in this whole building who had an extra play-off ticket to sell?"

Yes, wouldn't it be ironic? Dom's note seemed to dig into his thigh, reminding him it wasn't doing a bit of good hidden in his jeans. "Damn you, Mike."

There was a definite smirk tilting Mike's lips. "Yeah, why don't you just wait, boss? You have six whole days to find a ticket."

Domenic sent him a scowl. "Get to work!" He watched while Mike, convulsing with laughter, headed toward the center of the garden. And then Domenic aimed himself for the room.

TWO

The attendant smiled as Domenic approached, leading him to belatedly wonder what he ought to say to someone he'd been waving to for nearly three years. Before he could come up with the right thing, she greeted him with a surprisingly girlish giggle.

"My, but you're bigger than you looked from across the lobby."

"Anyone looks small, standing next to trees," Domenic answered with a grin.

She giggled again. The business chatter and paper shuffling around the break room table stilled abruptly while the women checked him out, and then resumed with a bubble-bursting briskness. So much for Mike's musing that the sight of Domenic's manly physique might coax one of the women into stealing his phone number. He sent the friendly attendant a wink and approached the bulletin board.

The woman Mike had pointed out still stood in front of the board, sipping at her coffee while she scrutinized each and every message. The scent of chocolate, almond, coconut wafted from her, as though she'd melted a candy bar into her coffee. More likely she drank one of those designer coffees to go along with her classy clothes. Domenic would bet his lunch money that no pasta sauce or baby drool had ever marked her dry-cleaned lapels.

She wore her thick honey-blond hair caught back with a wide silver barrette at her nape. Not a strand escaped the severe style. The white foam cup pressed against the lush fullness of her lower lip. No lipstick dared stain the cup. Domenic wondered if she wore that invisible glossy glop, or if maybe she had a man in her life who'd managed to convince her that the taste of melted candy bars beat lipstick hands down. Nah, she probably just refused to let any hint of femininity soften her professional appearance.

She cocked her brow in his direction, silently chastising him for staring at her. Her challenge didn't soften, even when Domenic sent her an appreciative grin. She was tough, all business and impervious to male admiration—definitely not his type. Mentally shrugging off any further attempts at flirtation, he swiveled to the board. And looked straight at the destruction of his hopes.

Desperately seeking Steelers play-off ticket!!!!!

He tore the note from the corkboard, not caring that its pushpin clattered to the floor.

"Son of a—" Most of the curse escaped before he remembered his surroundings and gritted his teeth. The damned note was . . . beautiful, eye-catching, and disgustingly effective. Little cartoon Steelers cavorted across the bottom. A tiny football spiraled toward a miniature goalpost. A few rows of seats had been drawn in, each filled with a cheering fan, except for one empty seat which the artist had somehow managed to make look forlorn.

Please put L. Duncan here! implored the note. It was the sort of computer-generated wonder Domenic's secretary might have come up with on the office system, if he would have asked for her help. He wished now that he'd asked. There didn't seem to be much point in posting his own plain-as-mud hand-printed plea on the board when L. Duncan's marvel would grab all the attention.

Except that L. Duncan's note wasn't posted on that particular corkboard any longer.

For all of two seconds, Domenic toyed with the notion of crumpling the note and replacing it with his own. Two seconds, and then his conscience kicked in, reminding him that there were some things more important than being at Three Rivers Stadium in person to watch the Steelers kick some Carolina Panthers butt. Damned if he could think of a single one now, though—especially when the back of his neck started prickling.

The room had gone quiet. Too quiet. He didn't have to turn around to confirm that his muffled curse had caused every woman in the room to shift her attention away from her pie charts to the vicinity of the bulletin board. From the corner of his eye he could see Miss Candy Bar staring at him with open curiosity.

He moved to stick L. Duncan's note back up, but halted his hand in midair. Too late, he remembered that the note's pushpin had fallen to the floor. All those remaining were shoved into papers of their own. He'd have to reshuffle the messages, but that would only raise everyone's curiosity over why he'd removed L. Duncan's note in the first place. Or he could play hide-and-seek with the pushpin that had fallen to the floor.

No way he wanted to bend over in front of a roomful of attentive women, not even to salvage his honor.

He swallowed another curse and jammed L. Duncan's note into his pocket. The meeting couldn't last all day. He vowed to restore the notice to its place of prominence on the board the minute he saw the women desert the lunchroom.

"It's a paradox, isn't it?" mused Miss Candy Bar, skewering him in place just when he meant to turn on his heel and leave the room.

Paradox. He couldn't remember the last time a woman had said a word like *paradox* to him, couldn't remember if anyone ever had, come to think of it. Of course, his thought processes weren't helped along when she smiled at him, when those lips he'd last noticed pressed against the foam coffee cup tilted upward in a dazzler of a smile he would have never expected. She didn't need either glossy glop or lipstick to enhance their natural color—or her femininity.

"Huh?" he croaked, a witty comeback sure to impress a woman who used words like *paradox*.

Her smile increased its wattage. But not because she was laughing at his tongue-tied response. If anything, he fancied he read a brief glimmer of kinship in her eyes. Eyes the exact misty green shade of lavender leaves.

"This." She waved her coffee cup first toward the bulletin board and then the lobby, scenting the air around them with chocolate, almond, and coconut. The aroma was the perfect complement to her voice, so rich and sweet, it could make a man ache to hear her call his name. "This place is practically a shrine to high-tech communication, but we still depend on sticky notes and a corkboard for the important stuff."

"Uh, yeah." Great. Now he'd managed to utter *two* nonsense syllables. If he kept up this pace, he ought to regain his regular level of glibness sometime around the year 2000. Thank God Mike wasn't there to witness his distress.

Domenic backed toward the door.

She set down her coffee cup and matched him step for step.

God, she was gorgeous, even if she wasn't his type. Her navy pumps looked so sensible that he knew they weren't responsible for the delicious in-and-out curves moving from her ankles to calves to knees. Her navy suit might as well have been a uniform, it was so deliberately designed for business wear, but her skirt shifted against her thigh when she moved, tightened across her belly with each step, and Domenic had no trouble whatsoever imagining her luscious in-and-out curves continuing up past her legs to her waist, to her breasts.

She cast a furtive glance toward the seated women, turning her head just enough to free one shimmering tendril of her hair. It fell beguilingly against her neck, brushing the slender silver chain she wore. A delicate hint of rose crested over her cheeks, natural, not like the fake blush some women applied with the diligence of a student taking the final exam in clown makeup school.

"I don't suppose you have it with you?" she whispered.

The scrambled eggs that Domenic used to call brains didn't seem capable of forming anything approaching coherent thought. So he said nothing, just edged another step toward the door.

"I have my checkbook right here." She patted a tiny purse that dangled from her shoulder to ride against her hip, and then something like panic flitted across her features. "Oh, that was silly of me. You'd prefer cash, I'm sure, and now that I think of it, cash would be much better for me too. There's an automatic teller machine out in the lobby."

A terrible suspicion flooded through Dom, followed hard by a sick lurching in the vicinity of his vitals.

The note he'd thoughtlessly torn from the bulletin board and stuffed into his jeans seemed to burn straight through the pocket.

"Don't tell me you're L. Duncan." He barely recognized the hoarse rasp as his own. *Please don't tell me you're L. Duncan,* he prayed.

"Oh, L. *Duncan*, pooh." She gave a dismissive flip of her hand, oblivious to the groan he couldn't suppress. "My friends call me Lynne. Actually, everybody calls me Lynne. Short names like mine don't inspire nicknames."

"Lynne," called one of the women from the table. "We're ready to begin whenever you are."

"See what I mean?" Lynne's nose crinkled. She lowered her voice conspiratorially. "I wouldn't exactly consider *her* a friend."

Domenic had the awful feeling that she'd soon demand he be the only person on the face of the earth to call her Miss Duncan.

"So, where's the seat you're selling? Not that it matters—I'll take it regardless of what section it's in." She looked up at him with such anticipation sparkling in those misty green eyes that he wanted to promise her, the pick of any seat in the stadium.

"Lynne." He spoke with every intention of admitting the truth then and there, but the way her name felt on his tongue, so soft and gentle, sort of sidetracked his determination.

So, too, did the circumstances. He couldn't stand there and admit that he'd copped her note, not while a roomful of her curious colleagues looked on and absorbed every word of their conversation. He couldn't imagine how he'd convince her that he'd truly intended to put the note back, not without explaining his reluctance to bend over in front of the women. He'd only come off sounding like a conceited macho jerk.

"Let's get out of here." He caught her hand, mentally adding an apology for outraging her sensibilities to his list of things to do once his brain started working. And then he couldn't think much at all, when she twined her fingers through his, and he would swear, really swear, that her thumb drew an almost imperceptible circle against his work-roughened knuckle. His blood roared in response.

"Lynne?" One of her coworkers half rose from her seat, as if she feared Lynne might need help.

"Start without me." Lynne answered with enough authority to make Domenic realize she outranked all those others at the table. "This won't take more than a few minutes."

It shouldn't have. He should have stopped right outside the room and explained everything. Instead, he found himself towing her straight for the sanctuary of the Atrium Garden, where the gently trailing branches and flourishing greenery might somehow soften his mistake.

She kept up with him—none of those mincing, tight-skirted steps for her. She moved with the swift, sure strides of the ladies who played basketball in their heels in the TV commercial.

"Hey, the cash machine's in the West Wing corridor!" she called as he charged across the lobby in the completely opposite direction.

"Hey!" she called once more, sounding decidedly worried, when he stepped over the low cedar-block decorative wall that edged the garden. She slowed, pitting her slight weight against his, and he knew she wouldn't take another willing step. Who could blame her? He'd been acting like an idiot from the first minute she'd seen him.

"It's all right." He turned to face her, aware of the battlefield symbolism of finding himself entrenched in his familiar garden, she on her own marble-tiled turf. The rose tint had deserted her skin, leaving her pale and apprehensive. He searched for something to say, anything, to breach the gap between them, something that might reassure her. "I'm the landscape architect. My helper's working somewhere in the garden right now."

"So there are two of you?" She jutted her chin toward the garden and then glared at him as if she suspected he and Mike might be serial killers bent upon ravishing her behind the ficus benjaminas. Dom figured her opinion of him wasn't likely to improve, considering the confession he was about to make.

She tugged, and he realized he still held her fingers entwined with his. He loosened his grip; she jerked free and stepped back, putting some distance between them. It was probably for the best, since it put her out of range if she decided to slug him after she learned the truth.

"Just sell me the ticket and we can go our separate ways."

"I don't have a play-off ticket to sell to you, Lynne."

She stared at him, unblinking. Her silence, when he'd expected an instantaneous spewing of righteous invective, unnerved him more than any well-deserved insult she could hurl.

Eventually she spoke. "Why did you take the note off the board if you don't have a ticket to sell?"

It didn't seem like a good idea to admit he'd been planning to post a note of his own. She'd never believe that he'd found himself so stunned to find her note so much better than his, he'd snatched hers up without thinking.

"Well?" she challenged.

"I don't know." Dom winced at his lame response. Hell, his four-year-old nephew had muttered the same words when his mother begged to know why he'd strewn the entire contents of her kitchen cabinets throughout the house.

"Why didn't you put the note back?"

"I meant to." Domenic cleared his throat. That, too, seemed like a subject it would be prudent to skirt. Besides, there was little point in trying to convince her of his innocent intent. Even if she believed him, it wouldn't lead to anything. "I meant to stick the note back up as soon as your meeting ended. Here, I'll just return it to you now." He dug it from his pocket and held it out.

She plucked it away with the lightning-fast reflexes of a she-wolf snatching her cub away from the edge of a precipice. Dom's fingers tingled, missing the feel of her hand clasped so trustingly in his mere moments before.

"I'm sorry, Lynne. I don't know what else I can say." He tried to imagine how he might feel if he'd caught someone removing his note. "Under the circumstances, I can't blame you for thinking I'm scum."

She tilted her chin a notch higher, which made her look rather fetching despite her obvious anger. A chin-tilt like that marked her as brave and determined, even if her severe hairstyle had loosened during their headlong rush across the lobby. The silver barrette clung only to a scant handful of honey-blond curls. The rest had fallen free to brush against her shoulders, silky and supple and shining beneath the pale winter light flooding through the atrium glass.

She glanced toward the note in her hand, and color returned to her cheeks. She snapped her head up, and this time Domenic was the one to take a step back, away from the fury that stormed in her eyes. "You! You're worse than scum! You're . . . you're *really* scum!"

Really scum didn't seem like much of an embellishment, not from a woman who used words like *paradox.* Domenic groaned when he saw the reason for her outrage. The note Lynne gripped in her hand wasn't decorated with tiny cartoon football players or miniature goalposts. It didn't beg someone to put L. Duncan in an empty seat. Plain and hand-printed, it urged someone, anyone, to call Domenic Corso if they had a play-off ticket to sell. He'd reached into the wrong damned pocket and handed her the wrong note.

"Well, Mr. Domenic Corso." She read from the note with a scorn that blunted any pleasure he might have taken in hearing his name on her lips. "This is really low."

Domenic rubbed his forehead. The pounding in his head told him that he must have secretly nurtured some faint hope that she might believe him. No chance of that now.

"I don't know what I can say, Lynne. Believe it or not, I just grabbed your note off the board without thinking it through."

Again, she answered him with silence. It seemed his admission had only worsened matters, for she now seemed wary of meeting his eyes. She worried her lower lip, and her fingers worked convulsively against her purse strap. Odd. Evasiveness, quivering lips, and nervous fingers all pointed to guilt or embarrassment, and that made no sense. Lynne had done nothing to feel guilty or embarrassed about.

"I'd do anything to make this up to you," he said quietly, hating that he'd even temporarily robbed her of her poised confidence.

"Anything? That's an awfully risky offer to make."

The tiny quaver in her voice encouraged him to embellish his vow. Hell, he figured, there was no point in being Italian if he couldn't exaggerate now and then.

"I'd get down on my knees and apologize if it would make you feel better."

"On your knees." She whispered his words back, so softly that he wasn't sure she'd really registered what he'd said. And then she lifted her head and treated him to a speculative smile, one that held more than a hint of her earlier verve. "Actually, there *is* a way that you could make this up to me."

"Anything," he promised, delighted. "Just name it."

"Getting down on your knees would be very appropriate." She postponed stating her demand but looked quite smug about the whole thing.

"What do you mean?" He held himself still, suddenly wary of both her equivocating and her restored humor. He could always anticipate what the soft, gentle, uncomplicated type of woman had in mind. He didn't have a clue of how a business barracuda like Lynne meant to strike.

Lynne was definitely looking perkier by the minute. Too perky. Domenic's instincts urged him to bolt as if pursued by a herd of charging buffalo.

"On your knees, Mr. Corso."

"Knees?"

"Of course, knees. That's the proper position for a man to assume when he asks a woman to marry him."

THREE

Domenic Corso turned rigid as a piece of garden statuary, complete with a gargoyle grimace. Not that Lynne could blame him—as soon as the words were out of her mouth, she'd frozen into her own impression of a concrete nymph.

Oh, God, she shouldn't think of words like "nymph" while standing in the aura of the sexiest man she'd met in ages.

Then, she supposed she ought to feel somewhat cheered that she'd managed to think anything at all. Her mind had gone numb after that interview with Susan, so numb that coming to grips with what she'd done felt like swimming through an ocean of ink toward a pale, insubstantial glimmer of light.

She glanced at her watch. "Fifteen minutes," she whispered in stunned disbelief.

Domenic scowled at her, silently demanding an explanation. He deserved one, considering the whopper of a lie she'd just enmeshed him in.

She bit her lip. So much for Susan's theory that taking risks opened new worlds of possibility. Lynne simply was not cut out for acting on impulse, for acting without weighing the consequences. She couldn't even sit in a chair without worrying how to place her butt, for goodness sake. So maybe she shouldn't be surprised that a mere fifteen minutes after resolving to test the waters of impulsiveness, she found herself trapped in a lie, surrounded by thoughts of nymphs and sex while proposing marriage to an utter stranger.

Susan would not be impressed.

It was obviously going to be a lot harder than she'd anticipated to get the hang of this risk-taking. She probably should have started on a smaller scale.

She moaned.

Domenic blinked at the sound, and then took a step back, retreating from her.

"You want me to ask you to marry me? I know I said I'd do anything, but don't you think that's a little . . . extreme?"

Part of her agreed, while another part got a little miffed that he obviously found the prospect so dismaying. "Don't worry. I have no intention of marrying you—or anybody else."

His relief manifested itself in a heart-stopping smile that involved his whole body. He relaxed, and his shoulders and biceps stretched the limits of his shirt. Interesting. Kind of fascinating, actually, but only because the men she usually dated did not lift heavy objects for a living, as this man so obviously did. His hip cocked a little, just enough to let the shirt button near his belt gap open, revealing an inch of pristine white T-shirt. Flat T-shirt. Not an ounce of spare flesh. All topped with a dazzler of a smile, a slash of white against the hint of smooth darkness underlying his flesh. He probably had to shave more than once each day.

Terrific. She'd taken her first risk by lying to a man who was probably an expert at wielding a razor. If Beth were there, she'd tell Lynne to look on the bright side—maybe Domenic would make a nice, neat slit when he cut her throat, so she wouldn't look too bad in her coffin. She'd go out while she was still a rising star, sort of like Buddy Holly, before people realized what a failure she was in danger of becoming. Maybe Susan would deliver a eulogy admitting that Lynne would have made one fine senior sales and marketing specialist.

"Lynne?" Domenic's deep, husky voice interrupted her morbid reverie. Voices that wrapped around you like silken threads didn't belong to the throat-slitting type at all. Too bad. Now she'd live—and have to admit her lie and endure the embarrassment.

Domenic Corso. She glanced down at the slip of paper clutched in her fingers, thinking that the bold slant of his handwriting suited him.

"Are you going to let me off the hook then?"

"Um." She swallowed. "Well, you don't really deserve to be hanging from a hook."

He quirked a brow. Then his smile broadened and he leaned toward her, just a little, crossing his arms and doing even more alarming things to his sleeves. "I realize you don't know me from the man in the moon, but I swear I don't usually do things like steal notes. I don't really understand it myself. I guess I let myself get too desperate. I behaved like I was possessed or something."

Lynne wished she'd thought up that theory first. Victims of demonic possession could be excused for wandering around in a mind-numbed daze. "Believe me, I understand how desperation can make a person do stupid things."

"Spoken like a true impulsive," he said with an easy grin.

"Goodness, no!" she said, horrified. "I don't have an impulsive bone in my body."

He treated her to a lazy sweep of his regard that warmed her everywhere it touched, making her wallow in thoughts of nymphs and sex all over again.

"A pity," he drawled.

Up until this morning, she'd taken pride in her careful planning, and now it seemed everybody felt obligated to point out she lacked genes for impulsiveness, like it was some kind of serious character flaw. "I'm learning how to take risks. I wrote it down at the top of my to-do list."

He coughed into his fist the way people do when they're trying to hide a smile. "Well, Ms. Duncan—"

"Don't call me that." She shuddered.

"Okay. Lynne. You're not impulsive. You just ask every man you meet to marry you, hmm?"

"Oh, that."

"Yes, that."

"It's my first attempt," she admitted.

"You got off to a good start. Getting married is risky business."

"We don't actually have to get married. We just need to apply for the license and—"

"Whoa! You're confusing the hell out of me."

She closed her eyes briefly. He was right. Ordinarily, she reviewed and rehearsed her proposals until she could stand up in front of a boardroom full of managers and present the most complicated projects with clarity and persuasion. Flying by the seat of her pants played havoc with her thought processes and proved what she'd secretly suspected: She could never let her emotions rule her head or disaster would surely follow.

She put a hand against her stomach to still the knot of distress quivering there. "My name isn't Lynne Duncan. It's Lynne *Stanford*."

"But the note said L. Duncan—"

"I know what the note said. But my last name is Stanford."

His eyes narrowed, and his sleeves did a little bulging as he whipped L. Duncan's note from his pocket and pointed it at her like an executioner's pistol. "This isn't your note, then."

"I never said it was."

She could almost see his mental processes at work as he replayed the few sentences they'd exchanged. "You tricked me."

She flushed.

"You called me really scum." Wounded pride rather than anger radiated from him. "You scared me half to death with all that talk of asking you to marry me."

Being scared half to death obviously wasn't as bad as having your world crash down around you. An easy grin tilted his lips, and he seemed to be in perfect control of his senses. Unlike herself. She'd behaved like an errant Ping-Pong ball since leaving Susan's office, bouncing blindly, caroming without direction, looking for a nice, safe net.

"I had a good and noble purpose," she countered. "I want to go to the play-off game on Sunday."

"So does half the city, which is why desperate people

like me and L. Duncan are trying to post notes on bulletin boards."

"And why desperate people like you and me are swiping them." She lifted her chin to disguise the way her face heated. Domenic cleared his throat uncomfortably. Well, they were both guilty of trying to deceive each other, even if neither of them was willing to admit it out loud.

She made a peace offering. "A woman in my office gave me the idea." She rushed to explain everything before he could turn her down. "The marriage license bureau chief announced he's going to raffle off his pair of tickets among the couples applying for marriage licenses today. When I realized you wanted to go to the game as much as I do, I figured, why not take the chance?"

"And since you had 'take a big risk' on your to-do list, here we are, right?"

She opted to ignore his humorous sarcasm—it struck too close to the truth. She tried to remember out loud the details Ellen had explained. "We don't have to get a blood test or anything. Just plunk down thirty-two dollars and fill out an application."

"You're kidding. People can just waltz in and apply for a marriage license? They don't have to pass a sanity test first or anything?"

She'd ping-ponged herself right into the clutches of a confirmed bachelor. His attitude suited her perfectly, so she couldn't understand the little pang of disappointment she felt. She ought to be relieved that his reluctance gave her a way to back out without losing too much face. "Maybe I ought to take a sanity test for suggesting this. Forget it. It was a stupid idea."

"Hold on. We've both agreed that desperation forces

people to do stupid things. You don't strike me as the type of woman who ordinarily gets desperate about football. What's the *real* story here, Lynne?"

He stood there, all warm and solid, staring at her with concern creasing his forehead. Rich, exotic greenery framed him from behind. The familiar bustling echo of the TechnoCenter surrounded them, somehow sealing them in a private cocoon. And suddenly she felt the urge, the *need*, to tell someone what a devastating blow she'd taken that morning.

She couldn't admit the truth to her colleagues—she'd grown up believing it was dangerous to reveal vulnerability to those who might have the same goals. She'd neglected her friends for too many months to feel comfortable calling and asking them to commiserate with her. She certainly couldn't admit her failure to her parents. They'd only exchange bitter little glances and shake their heads, telling her without words that she'd managed to disappoint them yet again. She had nobody to tell.

Except Domenic. There was something about him that made her want to lean against him and tell him that she hurt. That was silly—she couldn't bare the full depths of her despair to a total stranger. Her instincts whispered she could trust him . . . but then she wasn't so sure that she could trust her instincts. Judging by her current predicament, they didn't function so well without lots of advance preparation.

"Someone said . . . something . . . to me this morning that made me realize how much I'd missed out on lately. All of a sudden I realized that I didn't ever want to miss another football game."

She hadn't planned on being so honest. If he laughed at her she would die. But he merely looked puzzled and a little sympathetic. "Forget it," she said. "It's not important."

"You're not going to make much progress in learning how to take risks if you back off at the first sign of resistance," he said.

She scowled at him. He was right, damn him. "I didn't back off. I can always find someone else to do this if you're not interested. Men would probably jump at the chance once I explain that it's only sixteen dollars apiece, and the odds are thirty to one or better."

"Those are terrific odds," he said grudgingly.

"Outstanding odds," she agreed.

"There has to be a catch."

The old Lynne Stanford would have heartily agreed, and volunteered a weekend or two of unpaid overtime to study all the angles. The new, riskier Lynne that she'd vowed to become about twenty minutes ago quelled all caution. "The license expires in sixty days. There are no license police who come around to make sure it's used. If we win, we go to the game together. If we don't win, no harm done, and only sixteen dollars lost. Either way, we move on. Nobody will ever know."

He betrayed a hint of reluctant interest by gnawing at his lower lip. He shifted from one hip to another. Signs of a prospect ready to bite.

"Sorry you're not interested," she said. "Good luck finding a ticket." She swiveled on her heel. Slowly. Very slowly.

"Wait."

She paused and looked over her shoulder at him.

"Damn, this is hard." He stood there frowning, his arms crossed over his chest, looking for all the world like a condemned man who'd just been offered a choice between electrocution or lethal injection.

"You're afraid to do this!" At least she wasn't alone in that.

"You bet. I've spent thirty years avoiding the marriage license bureau. You won't sue me for breach of promise or something when we don't get married?"

She hadn't thought of that, but reassuring him was a simple matter. "Don't worry. Marriage isn't on my agenda just now. I'm up for a promotion, and I need to devote all my time and energy to earning it. I don't have time for a relationship. And that's why I couldn't ask one of my current men friends to do this—they might read more into it than I intended."

He blanched. "God, yes, that's true. I couldn't ask any of the women I know to do this without giving them the wrong idea."

"That's why it's best to do this with a total stranger that I'd absolutely *never* consider marrying." She ran a quick glance over him, taking in the jeans and work shirt. "I'd never marry you."

"You're not exactly the type of girl I'd take home to meet my mother, either."

"Well, then, you see," she said, pleased. "We're perfect for each other."

She glanced over at the break room. Beth stood in the doorway, alternately motioning for her and pointing to her watch. Lynne couldn't fault her impatience. She'd made such a fuss earlier about the snow delay, and now she was the one responsible for postponing the meeting even longer. She wouldn't make points toward that promotion if she let her practice risk-taking interfere with her job.

"Are we going to do this?" she asked Domenic.

He crossed his arms and expelled a little puff of air that stirred the lock of hair on his forehead. "I guess."

"Oh, brother, when I really get around to discussing marriage with a man, he'd better show a little more enthusiasm."

"Make up a spec sheet for your ideal man," Domenic suggested. "Put 'must show enthusiasm' right at the top of the list."

His sarcasm rubbed her the wrong way, especially since it sounded like a pretty good idea.

"Believe me, when I find the right man, he won't have to be instructed to be enthusiastic."

"When I find the right woman, my lady will be so worn out by my enthusiasm that she'll be begging me to let her have a little rest. But I won't."

"You won't."

"Nope. I'm a hands-on kind of guy."

She glanced at her watch to avoid looking at his hands. The time shocked her—she'd wasted far too many minutes batting verbal tennis balls with Domenic Corso.

"I'll be tied up in this meeting for a couple of hours, and my afternoon schedule's pretty tight too. That leaves lunchtime. I could catch the noon express and meet you at the courthouse around twelve-thirty."

"Actually, I'll be working here until around noon myself. We could ride into town together, if you don't mind riding in a truck."

"You wouldn't worry about that if you'd ridden a bus lately. Believe me, a truck will be a big improvement."

Things grew awkward between them then.

"So, I'll pick you up at the front entrance around noon, okay?"

The Whole Nine Yards

35

"Noon," she agreed.

He whistled a snippet of a haunting melody through his teeth, the way a person whistles when they're not thinking about what they're doing. A nervous habit.

"What's that song?"

"Oh." He flushed. "The theme from the movie *High Noon.* The words say something about lovers not forsaking each other on their wedding day."

"We're not lovers, and we're not getting married," she reminded him.

"The song just popped into my head. They must have televised that movie a hundred times a year when I was a kid. My mother watched it every time. My brothers and I used to sit around and tease her through all the sad parts, so she wouldn't suspect we wanted to cry too." A fond smile curved his lips, and Lynne wondered what it felt like to have memories that made you smile years after the fact.

Lynne could picture his memory with startling clarity—a miniature Domenic leaning back against an overstuffed chair in front of the television, trying manfully not to cry. A tear-streaked woman pressing a freshly laundered handkerchief to her eyes with one hand, while her other rested atop the rich brown curls of the sons clustered around her feet. Lynne didn't know where that strangely appealing image came from; she'd certainly never witnessed it in person.

"You know how kids like to agitate their moms when they cry during sad love stories," Domenic said, breaking the spell.

"Mother was much too busy to watch television with me."

"Oh." He studied her then, and she froze at the thundercloud of sympathy that darkened his eyes.

"Noon," she said brightly.

"Noon."

Domenic realized he'd never tapped the full potential of his dump truck until he held open the passenger door for Lynne while she climbed into the cab.

She hadn't buttoned her coat, and it fell open as she lifted her foot to the running board. Her skirt was just a tad too tight to give her the freedom of movement she needed to hoist herself up the high step. She balanced precariously on the ball of her foot. Her skirt hiked up and plastered itself around her bottom, and outlined the sweet curve of her thigh.

"Need a hand?" Dom asked huskily, knowing right where he'd like to plant it.

She shot him a knowing look over her shoulder. "That's all right. I'll just grab on to this." She curled her fingers around the armrest and pulled herself up, swiveling gracefully and dropping that delectable bottom onto the leather bench seat. He smiled in appreciation. He loved the way women always managed to end up with their thighs at an angle, their knees pressed together, one foot tucked under the other, their legs one long, alluring sweep.

"Okay, Domenic, I have it figured out."

"Huh?" He blinked.

"The seat belt. I figured out how it works. You can close the door now."

"I was just getting ready to do that."

"I thought so." She bent to fasten the belt, but not quickly enough to hide her smile.

Dom closed the door less forcefully than he wanted. Jesus, she'd caught him staring at her like some adolescent gas pump jockey polishing a pretty customer's windshield. No wonder she'd smirked. He rounded the back of the truck, and even though the tailgate was in place, he thumbed loose one of the restraining pins and slammed it back into place. Twice. He vaulted himself into the driver's seat and slammed that door too.

"Are you ready now?" she asked sweetly.

In answer, he cranked the ignition. His truck roared to life. She leaned back a little, no doubt unused to the power of such a large vehicle.

"Three hundred horsepower."

She cocked her head.

"The engine. Three hundred horsepower. That's why it's so loud and rough."

"Oh."

Well, it was obvious she wasn't the type to be dazzled by his knowledge of internal combustion engines. She wasn't his type at all. What the hell did women like her talk about? Hair. All women talked about hair.

"I see you trapped it again," he said.

"Trapped what?"

"Your hair. You got it all tamed and under control again. I thought it looked nice hanging loose."

She sent him a pursed-lipped glower that would've had the nuns from his Catholic high school lining up to take lessons. "In case you haven't noticed, I'm dressed for success, not for loose hair."

"Maybe a little loose dressing would enhance your risky image."

"Maybe we ought to listen to the radio."

"Good idea." He wondered what had happened to his conversational skills. It wasn't like him to get sarcastic with women, but then the women he liked conversing with didn't smart-mouth him into revealing his grumpy tendencies. "We can listen to CDs, if you'd prefer music. I have mostly oldies loaded in the cartridge, but I think there's a Mariah Carey and a Michael Bolton in there."

"How about some news?"

He'd never known a woman who preferred news over Michael Bolton. "Sure."

He pressed a few buttons and found the noon news on KDKA. He arrowed up the volume to mask the quiet in the cab while he steered them out of the parking lot. A few seconds later he guided the truck onto the expressway and had them heading toward downtown. Within minutes, they were driving between the fingers of shadows thrown by Pittsburgh's skyscrapers. The radio whined from interference.

"Listen!" Lynne punched up the volume.

. . . so ladies, if your man's a Steelers fan and he's been dragging his feet about applying for that marriage license, remind him that he has only a few more hours to get you to the courthouse. One of the lucky couples who apply for their marriage licenses today will win two seats for Sunday's play-off game against the Panthers . . .

"See," she said. "Now you won't have to ask the clerk if it's true or not."

"I wasn't going to do that."

"Oh?"

"I trusted you." Actually, it hadn't even occurred to him that the scheme might not be legitimate. Now that he thought about it, though, a woman with Lynne's brains was perfectly capable of tricking some poor sucker of a man into getting married. Which was why he liked his women sweet and compliant, not tough and sneaky. Well, maybe sneaky was a little too harsh. Taking advantage of that note, pouncing on that vague letter *L*, required quick thinking and more than a little brass. Domenic doubted he could have braved it out half so well. "I trusted you more than you trusted me."

"What's that supposed to mean?"

"I saw your friend watching from the lobby. She wrote down my license plate number, if I'm not mistaken."

A delicate hint of rose crested her cheeks. "You have to be careful these days."

He couldn't fault her precaution. "That's right. Women—even risk-takers like you—shouldn't climb into dump trucks with strangers." He fought the irrational urge to make her promise that she'd never climb into any vehicle with any man she didn't know well . . . and then the even more irrational urge to want to throttle any man she knew well enough to climb into a vehicle with. "There's the courthouse," he said unnecessarily as they inched past the stone edifice.

"Oh, look at that couple," she said, smiling wistfully.

Dom glanced over at what had her so fascinated and swore beneath his breath. Some show-off had hired a stretch limo to deliver himself and his girl to the courthouse. The girl stood blushing while the show-off heaped beribboned bouquets into her arms.

Lynne practically pressed her nose against the glass, sighing over the sight. He wondered if she was as acutely aware as he suddenly was of the sharp tang of chemical fertilizer, the earthy redolence of top soil, that permeated the truck cab. A woman like her was more accustomed to the richness of supple leather seats and the lingering waxy smell of a hand-rubbed finish. He jerked the wheel and almost plowed them into the glass facade of the Mellon Bank building.

"You can't park here on the sidewalk!"

"Don't worry. I designed the interior gardens here." He paused, but she didn't try to take a peek at the layout. He quelled his unexpected disappointment. "The cops are used to seeing my truck parked here. They'll think I'm inside working on the garden. They'll never suspect that I'm next door faking a marriage license."

"No, I guess they won't."

She slid out of the truck with no help from him, even though he hurried as fast as he could to get around to her side. Not that he was so old-fashioned that he thought it was a man's place to help a woman from his vehicle, although doing so carried the not insignificant benefit of getting a good glimpse of her legs. His type of woman understood that.

A good eyeful of Lynne's luscious limbs might have lightened his snarly mood. He glared at the limo as they hurried past and was glad for the biting wind that had both him and Lynne pulling up their collars around their ears and mouths. It was impossible to talk. Otherwise, he might have given in to his macho compulsion to point out that any fool could rent a limo for a hundred bucks, while his dump truck had set him back more than the cost of a fully loaded Lexus.

He was usually pretty careful about divulging that kind of information. Women tended to get dollar signs in their eyes and begin planning trips to the mall when they thought they had him snared. Not that he intended to get anything approaching snared with regard to Lynne Stanford, who dressed as if she could afford her own shopping sprees anyway. But he still felt like telling her about the dump truck. A businesswoman like her might understand his success on a different level, might appreciate how hard he'd worked to build the business from a teenager's after-school project into a thriving concern that had earned a place on the city's list of Top 100 Businesses.

He'd be glad when this application business was over.

He glanced at Lynne. She kept her chin tucked into her collar but her attention darted over to the limo, and he'd swear that her brisk, no-nonsense expression softened into wistfulness.

Maybe it wouldn't be such a bad idea to hire a limo when he *really* applied for a marriage license.

FOUR

The couple from the limo sat filling out their applications with their foreheads touching, taking furtive little pecks at each other's lips like a pair of lovebirds. Lynne promised herself she'd never act so sickeningly sweet when she came to apply for her real marriage license.

Maybe she *would* develop a spec sheet, a sort of to-do list of things to keep in mind when she really found the time to apply for a marriage license.

For instance, she would not sit on one side of the overheated, municipal-beige room and fill out her portion of the application while her real fiancé sat way over on the other side, the way she and Domenic were doing now. It looked too suspicious, as if she and Domenic had come merely to get in on the ticket drawing. Which they had.

She stole a glance at the clerk to see if she might be frowning at them for violating the sanctity of the premarriage ritual. She wasn't. She sat there with a disgruntled frown creasing her forehead, as if she'd processed too many applications throughout the course of the day. She sagged a little when yet another couple breezed into the room, but then rallied and shoved a clipboard at them.

"Uh." The new guy gulped. "This application doesn't obligate you actually to get married, does it?"

The clerk scowled at him. "I'm gonna kill my boss. No, you don't have to get married, but if you win the tickets you have to pretend. Mr. Kane'll be mighty ticked off if he thinks you're doing this just for the sake of those tickets."

"Oh, not us, heh-heh."

Looking greatly relieved, the guy sat with his bogus fiancée next to him. They giggled as they filled out the application together.

The clerk's warning chilled Lynne's positive attitude.

Domenic didn't seem to notice. He shifted in his chair, staring with interest at the new couple. Or maybe just at the girl, Lynne couldn't be sure. A hands-on kind of guy like him probably spent a lot of time staring at women. She hoped he wouldn't try to flirt. She felt a twinge of annoyance at the thought of Domenic's brown eyes snapping with invitation, and chided herself. She had nothing to be annoyed about. Well, maybe she did. Considering the mood of the clerk, she might just pitch them all out if she knew they were there under false pretenses.

Did you hear that? Lynne mouthed at Domenic.

"What?"

His voice seemed to bounce and echo off the drab walls.

Lynne surreptitiously sized up Mr. Faker and decided that it wasn't a prudent risk to raise his ire by screaming out loud her suspicions about his motives. Maybe she was getting better at assessing risks. The notion cheered her. If she'd made this much progress in one short morning, that promotion was in her pocket.

"Next!" the clerk called, and amidst giggles and shushing sounds, Mr. and Ms. Lovebird approached the desk. Using them as cover, Lynne gathered purse, clipboard, and coat and scurried over to Domenic.

"What were you saying?" he murmured.

"Just that we'd better not let that clerk know we're just pretending."

"Don't worry—I've come this far. I'm not going to mess up our chances now."

Our chances. She ignored the way his low, husky voice resonated somewhere deep inside her. She held the clipboard toward him. "Your turn."

"I hate filling out forms. You do it."

"All right, I'll do it, but not because you issued an ultimatum. I just happen to like filling out forms."

"I just happened to figure you might."

He sat there looking as though not one jolt of guilt or trepidation affected him. His long legs stretched out before him, and he kept his hands loosely clasped at the top of his thighs, just below a faded spot on his jeans. His jacket hung open, baring his dust-smudged work shirt. Lynne's fingers twitched with the urge to brush him off, but only because Ms. Faker kept darting interested glances toward Domenic's midsection. Another item to add to that hypothetical specification sheet: Her real fiancé would wear neatly pressed suits at all times, just like her father.

"What's your middle initial?" she asked Domenic.

"Don't have one."

"No middle name?"

"Nope."

She used her middle initial religiously. Everyone knew that a nice three-letter set of initials added impact at the bottom of a letter. Domenic's memos would end with a no-oomph, plain old DC . . . no oomph, but DC made her think of direct current, which probably accounted for the sizzling sense of electricity she felt now that she was sitting next to him. Her hand trembled a little as she filled in NMI for no middle initial in the appropriate blank.

"Date of birth?"

He told her. He was three years older than she.

"Address?"

"Two Haverton Terrace."

She held her pen motionless above the line for a moment. He hadn't struck her as the type to own a grand Victorian in the city's ritzy Shadyside section. "Wow," she said at last.

"It's a great house. Still has all the original woodwork."

She kept quiet. This was usually the sort of comment a man made right before inviting a woman over to inspect the artifacts under discussion. If Domenic thought he'd use the lure of fancy woodwork to invite her home for a little seduction, he'd be disappointed. She hated fancy woodwork. Well, not hated it exactly, but it would be murder hiring a cleaning lady to keep all those little grooves and spindles polished.

Domenic said nothing.

"Occupation," she read off the form, wondering why her voice sounded so thready. "I can fill that in myself—gardener."

He snorted.

"Gardening *supervisor*?" she offered, remembering that he'd mentioned an employee somewhere on the scene.

"Landscape architect."

"What's the difference?"

"About five years at Penn State and a half-dozen certificates hanging on my office wall."

"A little touchy about our job titles, aren't we?" she murmured.

"Nope. But you sure are."

"Me! I've never said a word to you about my job title."

"No, but you have a tendency to curl up like a little hedgehog when you're talking about something that hits home with you personally."

"Hedgehog!"

"Yeah, all spiny and bristly, ready to stab anyone who comes close."

"No I don't."

"Oh, yes you do."

"Don't."

"Do."

He stared at her, daring her to deny it again, and she felt the heat flame in her cheeks. They were bickering like schoolchildren, and with the deadly accuracy of a school yard bully, he'd zeroed in on her weakness. He was right about her being overly sensitive about her job title. She'd vowed to her parents that she would move into senior management before she hit twenty-eight, and unless she managed to change Susan's mind about the promotion, it looked like she would be failing to live up to her bold predictions yet again.

Even so, that didn't excuse her for so rudely lashing

out. "There's a great promotional opportunity coming up. I thought it would be mine, but my boss said she's not going to recommend that I get it."

"Ouch," he said, but with a warmth that told her he wasn't reacting to a hedgehog-style jab. "Not caring about promotions is one of the advantages of working for yourself. But I take it this is a good one?"

"All the way from mid- to senior-level management."

"Explain to me in English why it's so much better than the job you have now."

"More responsibility," she answered at once. "More people working under my supervision. If I get it, it'll put me right on track, where I'd always hoped to be by now."

"Yeah, but will you like the job?"

"Well, I . . ." She paused, nonplussed. She'd never worried about whether she'd like the jobs she aspired to, and to tell the truth, some of them hadn't been great fun. "It doesn't matter if I like it."

"It should. There should be something about your work that you like."

"I like selling. I'm good at it too." She stifled a smile, remembering how much she'd enjoyed selling Domenic on this marriage license scheme. "I like working with small companies to show them how our communications systems can help them. But I don't get to do that much fieldwork anymore. I'll do even less once I get this promotion."

"Then why is it so important to you?"

She hadn't realized that she'd stiffened and drawn away from him until he slanted a look at her and said, "Hey, it's not a radical concept that a person ought to enjoy his work."

"Do you enjoy yours?"

"Most of it." He inclined his head toward the clipboard. "I'm not too crazy about the paperwork, so I'm kind of choosy about the projects I accept. I never want to get so bogged down in office details that I won't have time to do a little hands-on work in the gardens."

"That's right. You're a hands-on kind of guy."

"I like to be involved." He shrugged. "I guess that makes me a little obsessive. I'll bet you are too."

"Obsessive is a good word," she said slowly. She wasn't willing to admit that being obsessed by the drive to succeed suddenly struck her as a lot less attractive than going to work because she loved what she did. She pounced on the next question with something like relief. "Mother's maiden name?"

"Grieco. Maria Grieco. I'm full-blooded Italian."

"Father?"

"Deceased." There was only the faintest quiver, but enough to tell her he felt pain.

"I'm sorry."

"He died a long time ago, but I still miss him. How about your dad—is he still alive?" She nodded and pointed to *Franklin T. Stanford* printed neatly on the appropriate line. "Good for you. It must be nice to have him around to lean on every once in a while."

"Oh, yes. We have a standing appointment for lunch every three months. He never misses more than once or twice a year."

Domenic looked at her. Just looked at her. She pretended to erase something from the form.

"Well," he said at length. "That application's a lot more thorough than I expected. Look now much we've learned about each other."

"You don't know anything about me. Nothing important."

"Oh really?" His comment ended on a rising note that made her suddenly worry what he'd picked up on. She ran a mental inventory, trying to remember what they'd discussed earlier. Nothing important—mundane stuff. Old movies with teary-eyed mothers. Job satisfaction. Quarterly lunches. Nothing. He didn't know anything about her.

He shifted in his seat and leaned forward. Before she could move away, his fingers brushed her jawline. "Don't worry, Lynne. Your secrets are safe with me," he whispered. It seemed impossible that such a tender gesture could come from hands so big, so broad. She quivered, wanting suddenly, fiercely, to melt into that gentle touch.

His fingers rested against her skin, holding her absolutely still. She felt warmth radiating from him, and her eyes were riveted, absolutely riveted to the genuine promise she read in his. Her secrets were safe with him. *She* was safe with him . . .

"Next!" barked the clerk.

"That's us." Domenic slid his fingers away from her, and she wanted to grab on, hold him there. He smiled and held those fingers up crossed, showing her that he wished them luck.

Lynne sat there for the space of a heartbeat, unable to believe she'd been so affected by his touch. Domenic Corso obviously thought that a woman needed to be coddled and coaxed through every risky venture—and she'd behaved down to his expectations. She wasn't going to give him the chance to do it again. She made a beeline for a spot at the far edge of the counter, while Dom sauntered toward the middle.

The clerk swung her head along the distance separating them. "What's this?" she grumbled.

"We're a little nervous," said Domenic. He made a quick lunge and caught Lynne around the waist. "It's not every day a guy applies for a marriage license, right, hon?"

Despite a fair amount of wriggling, and despite reminding herself that she'd vowed to maintain her distance, he soon had her tucked close against his left side. It felt like coming up against a wall. A warm, pliant, nicely muscled wall, just right for a woman her size to lean against and hear the rumble of his calling her *hon* pulsate right through her.

"Raise your right hands and face the flag," the clerk ordered. Changing position and lifting her hand somehow brought Lynne closer against Domenic. She wished she hadn't taken off her coat. She wished she'd worn heavy wool, layers of it, instead of a silk blouse and jacket. On second thought, polyester would be even better. Natural fibers were no barrier at all to her body's awareness of Domenic's warmth and solidity.

The clerk finished with them in a few minutes. All they had to do was swear that they were really the people they claimed to be, and that nobody had coerced them into applying for the license against their will. Lynne glanced over at Dom on that one, but he didn't flicker an eyelash. The clerk checked the photos on their drivers' licenses, and then they were done.

It felt all wrong and yet so right, standing there with Domenic's arm wrapped around her. Wrong to pretend, right to feel warm and safe. There was another item for her hypothetical specification list. When she really applied for her marriage license, her real fiancé would have to hold her exactly the way Domenic held her now.

And he'd have to put up a little more resistance than Domenic did when Lynne gently disengaged herself from the embrace.

"Well," Domenic said, when they escaped into the outside corridor. "That wasn't so bad. I have to hand it to you, Lynne. You're one creative, inventive lady, thinking up this little scheme."

"What . . . what did you call me?"

"Creative. Inventive." He tilted his head at her. "Those aren't insults, you know."

No, but the compliments struck her like bolts of lightning that fried away the remaining layers of numbness clouding her brain. She wasn't creative or inventive at all—she'd heard her parents bemoan her lack often enough. And now she'd gone and proved it by virtually stealing Ellen's plan. She'd stood staring at that bulletin board thinking *if only I can get to that football game, everything will work out*, as though getting to the game would repay her for all her sacrifices, as though showing up at the stadium would impress Susan into giving her the nod for the promotion. She'd been behaving like a frantic, headless chicken dashing madly about without the sense to realize nothing would be the same, ever again.

Lynne shook her head, not trusting herself to speak. Not able to speak. The same sense of suffocation that had gripped her earlier grabbed her by the throat again. She hadn't shown any initiative. Maybe she wasn't senior management material after all. Maybe that's why she felt so depressed, why she wanted to hurry outside to Grant Street so the biting sting of the winter wind would provide an excuse for the tears she felt welling in her eyes.

She never cried.

"Do you want to grab something to eat before we go back?" Domenic asked.

"Go back?"

"To the TechnoCenter. You know—the place where you work, where I left my helper."

"Oh! Actually, I . . ." She knew it would be a big mistake to climb back into that truck with him. A man who could immobilize her with one stroke of his finger was entirely too distracting, and she had to buckle down and concentrate. "I'll take the bus back. I, um, I want to pick up something at Kaufmann's." He looked skeptical. "Something's on sale," she added.

"Oh, well, if something's on sale."

She nodded.

He didn't offer to wait for her in the truck. Funny. She knew in her gut that he was the sort of man who coddled women and held open doors, who sat in the car listening to the ball game while his wife ran into the supermarket for a couple of T-bones. Maybe he understood she was more into microwaving low-fat entrées than firing up the gas grill.

"I guess this is good-bye, then," he said.

She felt compelled to contradict him, and didn't dare explore why she was reluctant to admit that it was over between them before anything had ever gotten started. "We might win."

"Right." He grinned suddenly, and her knees felt weak at that slash of white, those tiny lines crinkling at the edges of his eyes.

He turned away, took a step, and then slapped his forehead as though he'd just had a brainstorm. "I almost forgot—let's exchange telephone numbers." Her heart began tripping furiously. And then he added, "so we can call each other if we win."

"*When* we win," she corrected. Thinking positive was a surefire path to success. She bent her head and dug through her purse. He patted his jacket at various levels with loud, solid thumps that told her how sturdy was that flesh he was pounding. They both located business cards at the same time. She took his, wondering how a small cardboard rectangle managed to retain so much warmth. Domenic glanced down at her card and then shoved it into one of his pockets.

"If we don't win, well . . . let's go Steelers." He winked and then turned away, and within a few seconds his easy-limbed stride had carried him into the midst of the returning lunch hordes. Soon he was completely swallowed from sight, most likely from her life as well.

"Rah, rah, rah," she whispered.

FIVE

Lynne wriggled her shoulders and repositioned herself. She'd never before felt so uncomfortable in her ergonomically correct office chair. She blinked her eyes rapidly several times, but nothing seemed to help her focus on the weekly status report. She might as well have stayed home in bed, staring wide-eyed at nothing, as she'd done all the previous night.

Sleep might have come, she had to admit, if she'd allowed herself to close her eyes. But every time she did, she'd been plagued with the image of Domenic Corso. The way he'd openly admired her legs when she climbed into his truck. The way he'd lounged back in his chair and sent heavy-lidded, smoldering looks across the room at her while she filled out the marriage license application. A hands-on kind of guy who'd made very little effort to touch her. He made her aware of herself in a physical way, a female way, which had somehow made her more conscious of his, well, maleness.

Maybe it was the jeans. Business suits didn't hug a

man's hips or fade in strategic areas that led a tired woman to lie in the dark wondering what sort of underlying strain taxed that stout denim.

Sleepless nights were nothing new to her, but up until now they'd been work related. Some nights she chugged coffee while working on rush projects. And she'd learned never to review her personal goals right before heading for bed, because she just spent hours worrying about that upcoming promotion, and how failing to snag it would mean she'd never get back on track. Maybe that's what had happened to her the previous night. Those heart palpitations, that breathless sense that something had happened that would screw up her well-planned timetable probably didn't have anything at all to do with Domenic Corso and spending an hour in the marriage license bureau with him.

Too bad there wasn't some sort of daredevil school where a naturally cautious woman like herself could go to learn how to become impulsive in a benign, harmless sort of way. She'd been extremely fortunate in finding a guy like Domenic when she'd plowed so recklessly into this scheme. Domenic would never take advantage of her temporary insanity. Thank God nobody would ever know what she'd done. Maybe she'd look back on this one day and laugh—the fiasco had the makings of a good story to tell her grandchildren. Providing she found the time to meet a real husband and have a few real kids so those grandchildren had a chance to come along.

She was only twenty-seven. She had time.

"Lynne? Do you have a minute?"

Susan stood in the doorway with a folded newspaper clasped to her chest. She looked as impeccably professional as always—dark hair pulled back and secured with a tasteful clip, Anne Klein suit in a complimentary moss-green. It shocked Lynne to realize how closely she patterned her own professional appearance after Susan's, and she wondered why she'd never noticed before. She supposed she could credit Domenic and his cracks about freeing her hair and dressing to suit her newer, more risky image. "Come in," Lynne said automatically.

Susan seemed to be struggling to hold back a smile, which lent an unusually merry sparkle to her eyes and a friendly flush to her cheeks.

"I owe you an apology," she said when she was standing right in front of Lynne. She tapped the newspaper with a manicured nail. "You should have said something yesterday instead of letting me spout off about you having no personal life. I guess I just never noticed your ring."

"Ring?" Lynne repeated while glancing at the newspaper. The classified ads faced outward. Susan's fingertip pointed straight to a column labeled "Marriage License Applications." Rows of names lined up beneath the headline. Her eyes unerringly settled on the pair of names three lines down: *Corso-Stanford, Domenic NMI, Pittsburgh—Lynne M., Pittsburgh.*

An awful feeling sprouted in the pit of Lynne's stomach. Her left hand started to throb, specifically her ringless ring finger. She wrapped her hand tightly around her empty coffee mug.

She'd let herself remain tongue-tied for too long. The little light of anticipation dimmed in Susan's eyes, replaced by the distance that had grown so familiar. "Oh, sorry. I guess you didn't go for an engagement ring. Lots of people don't these days."

"May I see the paper?" Lynne croaked. Susan obliged.

Matters didn't improve up close. There it was, plain as day, the announcement that she and Domenic had applied for a marriage license. "They shouldn't be allowed to print personal business in the newspaper," she muttered.

"These are what they call vital statistics, and they're a matter of public record," Susan said. "Besides, it keeps men honest. They'd be applying for marriage licenses left and right if they thought it would help them score without anyone knowing what they're up to. Don't you read the newspaper?"

"*The Wall Street Journal*, of course," Lynne said. OmniCom paid for a subscription for each of its managers. She subscribed to the *Pittsburgh Post-Gazette* at home. She used to enjoy reading the local paper, but this morning's issue still rested on her hallway table, unopened in its plastic sleeve, the way so many of them had gone into the trash lately. She seldom found time to do more than skim the headlines.

Chalk up one more small pleasure sacrificed for her job, and now look at the trouble her single-minded pursuit had gotten her into. She'd never get the promotion once Susan learned how horribly Lynne had botched things. Well, there was nothing to do but come clean, admit her mistake, and hope she didn't get fired for showing poor judgment. She dropped the paper and thunked her forehead down onto her fists.

"Lynne?" Susan asked tentatively. "I thought you'd be happy. I know I would—at this stage of my life, I'd probably wrap my arms around myself and dance a jig if I'd finally found Mr. Right."

Lynne couldn't imagine smooth, polished Susan doing any such thing, but Susan's confidence lightened her mood a little. Susan smiled too. It had been a long time since they'd shared a joke, an honest-to-god girl joke. Her respect for Susan leaped ahead a few more notches. She'd been right when she told Lynne that she'd retreated and held everyone at arm's length.

"This isn't what you think. Domenic's no Mr. Right. This whole stupid scheme is my first stab at taking a risk."

"You're kidding. Oh, Lynne, please tell me you didn't jump into a premature marriage because of that little discussion we had yesterday."

All Lynne's instincts kicked into gear. This would be the perfect opportunity to smile, shrug, and say that yes it was all a joke. Instead, her mind's eye showed her Domenic's smile and recalled his warm encouragement when he'd told her she couldn't back away from risks at the first sign of trouble.

"I'll admit our discussion threw me for a loop, but it made me face up to some uncomfortable truths. For some reason, I got it into my head that everything would work out if I just managed to get to the football game on Sunday. So when I found out how badly Domenic wanted to go, I remembered what Ellen had said about the marriage license lottery. I . . . I copied her idea." She mentally girded herself to accept whatever punishment Susan deemed suitable to showing such a lack of imagination.

But Susan skipped right over it. "Lucky for me I have season tickets. Anyway, Ellen's plan tanked. Mark said no. They didn't get the license."

"They didn't? Oh, poor Ellen."

"Kind of ironic, isn't it?" Susan said with a grin.

"I never expected this newspaper notice." Lynne summoned another reserve of strength, knowing she had to confess the rest of her blunder. "We have no intention of marrying. I promised him nobody would ever know what we did. I'm going to have to tell him."

"Well, he must be a good friend to have gone along with it. He'll understand."

"He's not really a friend. I only met him yesterday."

"And you roped him into applying for a marriage license right off the bat?" Susan looked impressed. Lynne wanted to roll her eyes in exasperation. It figured. She'd always struggled to earn Susan's approval with her work effort, and all she had to do was engage in talk about men and marriage. "You'll have to give me some pointers—I can't manage to get a guy to call, let alone marry me. Can I have him when you're done with him?"

From nowhere came a little stab of jealousy. "He's not our type. He likes meek and mild women who keep their opinions to themselves."

"Oh. Well, maybe you're right. I'll keep looking. I'm only thirty-five. I have time."

Susan's comment jolted Lynne. Just minutes earlier she'd been consoling herself with the notion that she, too, had time to develop the romantic relationship that she kept pushing off into the future. She wished she could ask Susan how often she'd revised her personal timetable.

"There had to be something about the guy that made you think 'marriage license' when you saw him, right? I'll bet he's a hunk."

"Sort of," Lynne admitted reluctantly, thinking of those hip-hugging jeans complete with faded spot, and the way his shirtsleeves stretched over his biceps when he fought with the gearshift on his truck. And those hands, so wide and strong and yet capable of gentleness. The skin along her jawline tingled with the remembered feel of him, the warmth of his fingertips, the heated glow in his eyes when he'd promised her secrets were safe with him. "He'll do," she whispered.

"Uh-huh." Susan's eyes narrowed, the way they did when discussing closing strategy. "Job?"

"He has his own company."

Susan pursed her lips in a silent whistle. "Maybe he's not the wrong type after all. Let me know when you cut him loose."

"You're welcome to him," Lynne said easily. But the minute Susan turned her back, she stuck out her tongue and made a horrible face at her.

Oh, God, her maturity had deserted her along with her common sense.

Susan had left her newspaper behind. With the index finger of her ringless left hand, Lynne traced their line, hers and Domenic's. *Corso-Stanford, Domenic NMI, Lynne M.* Corso-Stanford, *C* and *S* following each other in alphabetical order. Maybe that was why it felt sort of right, seeing their names lined up like that, rather than as Stanford-Corso, the way it would look if she really married Domenic and hyphenated her last name for professional purposes . . .

Oh, God. She dropped the paper and thunked her forehead into her fists again.

She wondered if Domenic was slumped at his desk in a similar position of despair. Maybe not. Maybe he didn't know yet that their harmless, nobody-will-ever-know secret was considered such a vital statistic that it had to be printed in the newspaper for the whole city, the entire metropolitan area, to see.

For her parents to see.

She deliberately quelled that thought. Mother and Father read *The Wall Street Journal* and a few financial newsletters. She was probably safe there for a while.

But Domenic . . . She had to call him and warn him, apologize right away before he found himself blind-sided by the news the way she'd been. She lunged for her purse and rummaged for his card. She tried to ignore the little surge of excitement that pulsed through her, and then decided it wasn't excitement at all, just nerves. This risk-taking was murder on nerves.

"Corso Landscape Designs," answered a crisp, efficient female voice.

Disappointment knifed through her at the realization that she'd gotten his office. Well, what had she expected—he'd given her a business card. Just as she'd done.

"May I speak to Domenic?"

"I'm sorry. Mr. Corso is out at a job site and not available. May I help you or take a message?"

Her news wasn't the sort Lynne wanted to leave in a secretary's hands. Come to think of it, it wasn't the sort of news she ought to deliver over the phone. It would be much better to serve it in person. Lynne checked her watch. She had a management team meeting at nine, and with luck would be free around noon.

"Could you tell me where I might find him? I'd like to meet him for lunch."

The secretary's voice frosted noticeably. "I'll be happy to give Mr. Corso your message, but I can't promise he'll call in time to make lunch arrangements."

"I understand. Please ask him to call Lynne."

A quick, indrawn breath was followed by a pregnant pause. "Lynne?" squeaked the secretary. "As in Lynne M. *Stanford*?"

Domenic's secretary knew her name. The full name, as printed in the newspaper. She was already too late. "He has my number."

"I'm sure he does." The secretary's voice warmed. "On second thought, I'll bet he wouldn't mind if you met him for lunch. He's checking out the gardens at the Lynch Park Mall to see if he's interested in submitting a bid. He should be there until at least two."

Lynne dug her meeting notes out of her briefcase and told herself that the excitement she felt was from knowing she had her morning presentation down pat. There could be no other reason why she felt like wrapping her arms around herself and dancing a jig.

Domenic leaned back against the wall, enjoying the scent of chocolate chip cookies wafting from the Mrs. Fields kiosk. He held his clipboard tucked between his arm and side—no need to take notes while watching this crowd. No wonder the management sought a change. Mall greenery ought to make people comfortable, encourage them to slow down, invite them to sit and rest and rebuild their strength for more shopping. Instead, most of these patrons rushed through the halls with scowls creasing their faces, others meandered to kill time, a few sat at badly placed benches, looking either exhausted or impatient. Nobody paid the slightest attention to the mall's expensively groomed landscaping—except for one woman, who made her tentative way along the edges of the largest garden area, peering between leaves as if expecting to catch Tarzan yodeling through the branches.

He figured her for a competitor. He knew the mall was soliciting other bids, even though the director had pretty much confirmed that the job was Domenic's if he wanted it. That took all the fun out of it. He preferred the challenge of coming up against a formidable foe.

His potential foe was well and expensively dressed in a taupe business suit and heels. She had her coat draped over one arm and clutched a paper bag in her free hand. She got too close to an overgrown diffenbachia. It tugged at her hair, freeing a shining honey-blond strand to curl against her neck.

Domenic pushed away from the wall. "Lynne?"

She didn't hear him call her name, not over the Muzak, the squeaking stroller wheels, the crying babies and shushing mothers, and several hundred pairs of shoes scraping and clopping against marble tile. A good landscaping plan would have swallowed some of the din. He made a mental note to make a real note about the noise reduction factor on his clipboard. Later. For now, he found himself striding toward Lynne Stanford and wondering what the hell she was doing there, obviously searching the landscaping when only guys like him tended to be found in such places.

"Lynne?" he called again when he was closer.

She turned quickly, and a glorious smile lit her face. Lit her. That was the only way he could describe the glow that kindled in her smoky green eyes and lent her smile a pure radiance. The sight of that smile did weird, troubling things to him, striking him speechless, for one, which seemed to be a particular hazard when facing this woman. Which turned out to be okay, because within seconds she seemed to get a grip on herself and her glow faded. A cool, unreadable business face came over her. Thank God for that business face. Otherwise, he might have said something dumb, like "Hey, you look really beautiful when you smile."

"I brought lunch." She held up the brown paper bag.

She'd brought him *lunch*? "Great. We can grab one of the tables in the food court."

"They have a food court?" She glanced down at her bag with what looked like embarrassment.

"One of the best. A lot of people shop here just because of the food court."

"Oh. Well, I don't shop. Except for emergencies."

"Like yesterday."

"Yesterday?" Puzzlement furrowed her brow.

"Yesterday—you couldn't ride back to the TechnoCenter with me because something was on sale at Kaufmann's."

She blushed. Ha! He'd pegged her right. She'd lied about that little shopping excursion, probably thought that showing up at work in a truck would be bad for her image.

"Oh, that was unusual for me. I find it so much more efficient to shop through mail order catalogs." They walked toward the food court. "Plus, there's Home Shopping Network and QVC. I usually tune in one or the other for background noise while I'm working at home. That way if I catch something interesting, I can just call in and order. Press a few buttons and the package comes in the mail—you don't even have to talk to a real person."

Domenic, no fan of shopping himself, still thought

he'd rather haunt malls than sit alone concentrating on piles of paper while some slick salesperson hyped cubic zirconia in the background.

"Doesn't that take all the fun out of spending money?"

"Fun?" She blinked, looking so adorably puzzled by the notion that he couldn't help embellishing.

"Fun. I thought women loved trying on all those soft and silky clothes, so they can torment their boyfriends by pretending to ask for their opinions." He swallowed, imagining Lynne Stanford stepping disheveled from a dressing room clad in clinging silk instead of no-nonsense wool, imagining her pirouetting and smiling for him while soft, slippery cloth floated and settled around her long and luscious limbs.

She sniffed dismissively and aimed straight for an empty table.

She plunked her purse down on one chair and then busied herself with the contents of the bag. She set out napkins and plastic spoons, and then carefully lifted plastic cups onto the table. Dom's appetites, all of them, surged in response. Who said a man had to come home to a home-cooked lunch everyday? Oh, yeah, his brothers. But then they'd probably never had the experience of a woman like Lynne Stanford spreading the table with store-bought delights like . . .

Nonfat yogurt.

Herb tea.

And two goddamned rice cakes.

"Caramel," she enthused, waving those hockey-puck-like things in his face while the scent of sizzling sirloin and melting provolone attacked from the Steak Hut, and the Mrs. Fields chocolate chips drifted over from the opposite side.

"Very healthy." He nodded at their table while his stomach rumbled in protest. "My arteries thank you."

She pinkened and shot him a pleased little smile. "I'm glad you like it. I brought double of what I usually eat so I could just save half for tomorrow in case you preferred something else."

"Very efficient," he said unhappily. If he'd been honest with her, he would have been able to order a steak hoagie without disappointing her.

"I'm not used to feeding men," she said with a soft, little smile.

Obviously not, although a man's lips could certainly find a feast if allowed to travel over her petal-smooth skin beyond the few inches revealed by her suit. He forced that thought away, only to have it replaced by another, equally intriguing one—she'd obviously come looking for him.

He peeled the lid from his yogurt container. He vaguely remembered his mother and sisters stirring yogurt, turning it from an unappetizing white to an unappetizing pink before they ate it. He stuck his plastic spoon into the cup, but despite his vigorous efforts, it still looked like elementary school paste. He glanced at the label—vanilla. "So what brings you here, besides the urge to feed me?" he asked with false casualness.

Lynne didn't stir her yogurt, but she stared longingly at it as if she wished it would turn into a whirling vortex and suck her out of there. "Oh, um," she said. "How's your yogurt?"

"You know what they say—vanilla's the world's most popular flavor," he said. "How did you find me?"

"Well, um." She spooned a minute portion of yogurt into her mouth. He waited while she swallowed, trying not to think too much about the way her mouth and throat worked over the easy task. She sent him a nervous smile. "Don't blame your secretary for telling me where you were. This is an emergency."

"Sounds serious."

"I'm . . . I'm not usually so tongue-tied."

He could think of lots better ways than vanilla yogurt to tie up her tongue. He jammed a heaping spoonful of the yogurt into his mouth.

"Oh, Domenic." He barely had time to register how nice his name sounded coming from her in such a soft, breathless rush, when she added, "everyone knows what we did. Our marriage license application was in the newspaper."

He sat there feeling like an idiot with his mouth full of yogurt and a plastic spoon sticking out of it while a sense of doom settled over him. But the good thing about yogurt was that while it might taste like crap, it was easy to swallow. "You mean some reporter wrote a story about us?" he managed to croak eventually.

"Not exactly. Did you ever hear of things called vital statistics?"

"Yeah." He let his gaze sweep over her, figuring her vital statistics to be in the neighborhood of thirty-five, twenty-five, thirty-five.

She noticed and drew back with a semidisgusted look that he knew he deserved and so didn't mind. "Municipal, or legal vital statistics—I don't know exactly why they're so vital. But they publish a column every day in the classified section of the *Post-Gazette*. It lists everyone who filed for marriage licenses, divorces, stuff like that."

He swallowed a curse along with a slug of his peppermint tea.

She bit her lip. "I know. I promised you that nobody would ever find out. I'm sorry. I didn't know about the vital statistics either."

He waved his hand in absolution. "It's not your fault. I knew there might be some repercussions, but I had promised myself that I'd do anything to get to the game, no matter how bizarre. I'm just worried about my aunt Rosa."

"Your aunt Rosa?"

"Yeah. She reads the paper from cover to cover. She starts with the Death Notices so she can be the first to break the news if anyone known to the family passes on. Next she works her way through the Help Wanted section trying to find a job for my loser cousin Vince. She should hit the classified ads by midday. I just hope she doesn't have a heart attack when she sees that listing."

As if his words were a cue, a muted telephone ring sounded from his jacket pocket.

"You have a cell phone?" she asked. Her business face shuttered her expression as he pulled the phone from his pocket. "You just gave me your office number."

"I don't even know this number. June—she's my office manager—is the only one who has it. Oh, and my mother—but she knows not to call me except for emergencies. If I handed out my number to everyone in my family, I'd never have time to get any work done." He glanced at the caller ID screen and once more cursed beneath his breath.

"June?" she asked hopefully.

"My mother."

"Oh, God, we're in trouble. She found out about us already."

We're in trouble. The phone demanded Domenic's attention, but he barely noticed its ringing over the echo of Lynne's words. *We're* in trouble. They were in it together, the way he and his best friends used to join forces to hide their childhood pranks from their parents. She stared at him with complicity widening those misty green eyes, and he wondered how long it had been since he felt that sense of companionship with another person.

I've been lonely for something like that, he thought. And that didn't seem possible, not with the hordes of relatives who usually surrounded him. He'd been dubbed the unofficial head of the family ever since his father died, and nobody seemed to notice that he got tired of the responsibility sometimes.

"Aunt Rosa must have done some speed-reading today and got on the horn the minute she spotted our names."

"Maybe not. Maybe it's just an emergency."

He couldn't help grinning at catching himself hoping the same thing. Some pair they made, hoping that a matter of life or death was at stake rather than the discovery of their little scheme.

"Oh, God, I'm sorry." She reddened with mortification. "I didn't mean that the way it sounded."

"I know. This whole situation makes me feel nervous too." The phone shrilled again. "I can't answer that now. I have to give myself a few minutes before I talk to her."

"You'll tell her the truth. About us . . . not being 'us,' that is."

"You bet." That elusive sensation of being close to her evaporated. While he had been savoring the possibility of feeling connected to her, she'd been fretting over how much time this was taking away from her job. He had to stifle a laugh. He couldn't think of anyone less likely to relieve his loneliness than uptight, single-minded Lynne Stanford.

He couldn't understand why he all of a sudden felt lonelier than ever.

The phone gave one final chirp and subsided into silence.

He set the cell phone alongside his rice cake and frowned morosely at them, not able to decide which he found less appealing. He toyed with them both, and it took a few moments for him to realize how intently Lynne stared at his hands.

He could almost feel the stroke of her gaze as it moved from his wrists to his fingertips. He remembered the way her hand had felt when he'd held it in his the day before, so fine-boned and delicate within his work-hardened grasp.

Well, he had workingman's hands, there was no hiding the broad palms and tough knuckles, the calluses padding his fingertips. He would expect a woman like her to be put off by their roughness. Instead, she stared with her head cocked a little to the side, as if she could imagine his big hands coaxing a tender seedling from its nursery bedding, or any of the other myriad chores he took pride in doing.

A wave of desire crashed into his core. Of all the come-hither glances he'd ever received from a woman, none had ever affected him as much as Lynne's contemplation of his hands. Nor had he ever been so conscious of them, of all that he asked them to do. Usually, around a woman, he had only one use for his hands.

"How did your parents handle the news?" he asked.

Her skin tone paled into a good imitation of vanilla yogurt. "I don't know if they heard about it yet."

"You came looking for me before calling them?" He couldn't help feeling pleased that she'd thought of him first, even though he knew she'd meant nothing by it.

"It's not going to be a pleasant conversation. They'll be . . . disappointed. My mother, especially."

Dom's elation deflated. Stanford women, it seemed, were quick to jump the gun when it came to forming negative opinions about him. But Lynne surprised him.

"It has nothing to do with you, Domenic. She'll look at it as a miscalculation on my part. She'll worry that I repeated all her mistakes by getting romantically involved before establishing myself in my career."

"Mistakes?" he asked softly.

She blushed. "Oh. Well, Mother could have moved much further ahead in her company if she hadn't gotten married and had a child before she'd moved into senior management. I sort of promised that I'd postpone marrying until I got that corner office. I just never expected it to take so long, and, well, she's concerned that I'm not motivated enough."

There was a world of hurt in her voice, the echo of a child who'd grown up feeling responsible for derailing her mother's ambitions. How much of Lynne's own drive, he wondered, stemmed from the need to prove to her parents that she'd been worth the inconvenience? Covertly studying Lynne's haunted expression, he vowed that no child of his would ever feel even slightly unwanted. Which was why he had to buckle down and find himself a warm, open, and contented lady to mother his future family.

"Things were different back then, Lynne."

"Not so different. It still takes a tremendous amount of work to maintain a relationship. I've watched other people—women *and* men—get derailed. It's far better to get to where you want to be and then let everything else fall into place."

"Postpone happiness, in other words."

"Happiness is relative and doesn't always last."

"Neither does a title painted in gold leaf on a mahogany door."

She tightened her jaw stubbornly. She obviously bought into her parents' jaded views on marriage and family. He couldn't understand why her attitude disappointed him—he'd had her pegged right from the beginning.

"You deal with your parents as you see fit," he said. "Right now, I have to call my mother, and I have a real bad feeling about this."

"You don't strike me as the type of man who's afraid of his mother."

There it was, that snippy little edge to her comment that told him she was lashing out against her own fears. At least they had one thing in common: They both dreaded confronting their parents with what they'd done.

"Lynne, *everybody's* afraid of my mother. But I have to tell her the truth before she starts baking pizzelles for the wedding."

Dom punched out the numbers with the enthusiasm of a hostage being forced at gunpoint to enter the code that would arm the doomsday bomb. He stole a glance at Lynne who sat there tidily spooning her yogurt, fueling herself for a long stint of memo writing or whatever the hell she did all day. Stroller-wheeling mamas crisscrossed behind her. No question which type of girl his family expected him to marry. The same type *he* expected to marry. "Here goes."

His mother picked up in the middle of the first ring. "Hey, Ma," he began, but that was as far as he got. He grimaced and held the phone away from his ear so Lynne could hear the torrent of Italian pouring from the earpiece. "Yeah. No. It's not . . . no, Ma, listen . . . yeah, no, I'll ask, no, wait, wait, wait, no Ma, no . . . No!" A click, followed by blessed silence.

With a sigh, he pressed the "end" button.

"You didn't tell her," Lynne admonished.

"I tried. You heard her—I couldn't get a word in edgewise. So you know what that means."

She drew back, looking frightened. He didn't blame her.

"I hope you're free for dinner tonight, Lynne. I have to take you home to meet my mother. You're not going to like each other very much."

SIX

She drove a BMW convertible. A two-door stick shift. The ultimate yuppie dream machine.

He drove a Honda Accord. A four-door automatic with dual air bags. The number one family car in America.

Dom figured that some psychological type might point out how their respective choice of vehicles proved their ultimate incompatibility. He didn't need to drop a hundred bucks on a session with a shrink to know that—he need only replay their conversation in his mind, and listen again to those luscious lips telling him what Lynne Stanford thought was important in life.

She believed that love, family, children, all were secondary to a career—he thought the most important thing about a career was the ability it gave him to provide well for his family. She believed happiness came from earning an office on the senior management level—he believed happiness came from surrounding himself with his loved ones.

Screeching tires and the blare of a horn from the next lane warned him to keep his eyes and mind on the road, or his incompatibility with Lynne wouldn't be an issue for long. He glanced into his rearview mirror, still not able to believe she would be there behind him. But she was. Damn, she sure handled that car well. She zipped along right behind him through each lane change as he led her down the highway to the Edgetowne exit. She didn't have to come. She could have let him face his family on his own.

Most women would, at least the women he usually dated. He gravitated toward sweet, loving creatures without an ounce of backbone, women who were content to let him take the heat and solve all their problems. Having a woman stick up for him was a new experience. Lynne might like to pretend she was all business, but doing things like this proved there were a few dents in her cold and indifferent shell.

He wondered if she'd talked to her mother and father since leaving him at the mall. It couldn't have been a pleasant experience explaining what she'd done, considering what she'd revealed to him about their disappointment in her. But she hadn't asked for his help. A guy who sometimes chafed against being called on to soothe every tiny wound shouldn't feel so left out just because someone—a stranger, really—handled things on her own.

He cursed under his breath when he turned onto his mother's street and saw the lineup of cars parked against the curbs. Mama must have invited every breathing family member. He was tempted to lead Lynne straight on through the neighborhood so they could continue their highway chase. That was about the extent of any relationship he could have with her anyway—moving, but never touching, aiming for a dream just beyond the horizon.

He slowed down and motioned for Lynne to take a parking spot close to the house. It took him a few more minutes to find a space a couple of blocks down. She had plenty of opportunity to make a run for it, but she was standing outside her car beneath a streetlight, waiting for him.

Waiting for *him*.

She stood with her arms crossed over her breasts, her chin tucked low into the scarf wound around her collar, her breath frosting the air around her. He wanted to rush up and wrap his arms around her, press her tight against himself, get them both warm for the ordeal to come. *Stop that*, he warned himself. This was sort of like a business trip for her, a deal gone sour that she felt obligated to rectify. She'd probably checked her watch a dozen times already, wondering what was taking him so long.

"Ready?" he asked a little huskily.

She nodded.

He angled his chin toward the long line of parked cars. "I have to warn you, it looks like the Corso clan turned out in full force."

If he had any doubts about her motivations for being there, she dispelled them. "Maybe that's for the best. We'll make our announcement once, and it will be all over with." She said that with her business face, and he knew it appealed to her sense of efficiency that she wouldn't have to spend any more time than necessary convincing his family she wanted nothing to do with him.

Their feet crunched companionably against the frosted sidewalks. He mentally girded himself for battle. He'd brought women home before, of course, but never with the slightest hint of marriage involved. Come to think of it, he'd pretty much stopped inviting women to his mother's house. They tended to cling a little too much, which probably wasn't a fair criticism, since walking in on his tight-knit family could be intimidating.

Not for Lynne. She had her chin tipped right up there while challenge snapped in her eyes. He'd told her she might not receive a warm reception, and in typical Lynne Stanford style, she meant to bulldoze her way right in. He remembered her telling him how much she enjoyed selling—well, she obviously intended to march in on his family and sell them on the truth. She kept her arms wrapped around herself, declaring her independence from him, which paradoxically made him want to pull one of her hands through the crook of his elbow, signifying their unity. He shoved his hands into his pockets.

A muted din vibrated from his mother's house. Even with all the doors and windows tightly closed against the January chill, he could catch the sound of voices raised high, of children shrieking with excitement. Lynne's confident stride faltered just a little. Her eyes looked huge and startlingly green against the pale porcelain of her skin—but maybe it was just the weird glow from the streetlights. She shivered—but maybe it was just her natural reaction to the cold.

He jammed his hands deeper into his pockets because he had the strangest urge to put his hands on her shoulders and pull her back against him, so they could breach the door together. He felt like protecting her, and she wasn't the sort of woman who required protecting. She was bold, strong, and capable. She'd probably stab her heel into his foot if he tried.

But damn, he wished she didn't look so pale.

He paused with his hand on the doorknob. "It's not too late to change your mind about going in."

She squared her shoulders and gave him a quick nod. "Let's go."

A little kid who grew up believing she was unwanted could withdraw into self-pity, or she could push her way past her parents' indifference and demand their attention. A girl who'd been repeatedly told she was a disappointment could self-destruct, fulfilling the prophecy, or she could become so determined to succeed that she was willing to put her personal happiness on hold to prove everybody wrong. Lynne Stanford, doggedly scheduling those quarterly lunches with her father, and pursuing her promotion without regard to her emotional needs, refused to withdraw or crumble. Push her and she pushed back. Tell her she couldn't do something, and she'd devote herself heart and soul to proving that she could.

She possessed some great traits to pass along to her kids, providing she ever found the time to get married.

They were a team, for this night at least. The way they'd formed a team to try to win those football tickets. Strange. He'd spent maybe one hour total in her company, and already they'd joined forces on going after those tickets, facing down his family—two massive challenges that he wouldn't have dared tackle with anyone else.

He felt a little surge of pride in her that raised all sorts of warning bells within him. He had no business feeling protectiveness and pride for a woman who meant to burst in on his family and tell them all that she wanted nothing to do with him.

Not that he wanted anything to do with her, either.

He opened the door.

The sound hit them like a wall, bringing them up short within the frame of the doorway. From the front entrance, it was possible to see straight through from the living room into the dining room and then the kitchen. The rooms all opened up into each other, creating one vast space, a space which was packed wall to wall with Corsos of every age and size. The cold draft from the open door eventually drew everyone's attention. Silence struck as suddenly as if someone had pushed a mute button.

His grandmother—oh, hell, he couldn't believe his *grandmother* had left her house for this—turned from the sink and stared. Her shrewd gaze skipped over Lynne's blond hair and smoky green eyes, and when Grandmama's jaw tightened Dom knew she'd silently and accurately assessed Lynne as not possessing a drop of Italian blood.

Someone, one of his idiot brothers no doubt, let out a low wolf whistle.

"You make a nice couple, Dom," called out one of his sisters, and then the bedlam resumed.

He braced his legs.

A horde of small children hurtled themselves at his knees, screeching with delight and crying, "Uncle Dom, Uncle Dom!" He didn't bend to roughhouse with them as he usually would, because his three brothers and two brothers-in-law had lined up and were checking Lynne out, and it took all his concentration to keep from socking them in their leering jaws.

His sisters and sisters-in-law swarmed around Lynne before she even had a chance to take off her coat. Someone shoved a baby into her arms. She blinked at the infant, who blinked back, turned red, and then let out a huge squall. Lynne looked so stricken that one would've thought she'd been handed a space alien instead of a shrieking, bald minihuman.

"No thank you," she said graciously, handing the baby right back.

His mother and grandmother exchanged appalled glances.

Well, if he'd nurtured the faintest hope that her unhappy childhood had left her longing for kids and a family of her own, she'd effectively killed it then and there.

His mother had stolen up on him while he was watching Lynne prove she could never fit into his world. Mama tugged at his sleeve. "Introduce me to your girlfriend, Domenic."

"She's not my girlfriend."

"Sure she's your girlfriend. Come on everybody, meet Domenic's girlfriend."

"I'm not his—" Lynne called.

"She's not my—" Domenic bellowed.

It was no use. The din escalated into a roar of well wishes, congratulations, comments about Domenic's slyness in keeping Lynne hidden from them for so long.

They would have exhausted themselves eventually—like in about four hours—but Dom could tell from Lynne's panicked expression that drastic measures were called for. He forged his way out of the kids' clutches and through the phalanx of women surrounding her. He touched her shoulder and bent low so he could whisper in her ear. His lips accidentally brushed against her hair. For a minute he lost his train of thought. She smelled good, a heady combination of fresh winter air and faint perfume. "Don't worry. I know how to get this under control."

"I don't know," she said doubtfully. "They don't seem to pay much attention to you. Maybe I ought to try."

The very idea that she was willingly offering to tackle his family sent an odd little pleasure zinging through him. Everyone—especially the people in this house—expected him to handle everything on his own. Not that he minded. But it might be nice if, once in a while, someone offered to take on a little of the dirty work. He smiled and squeezed her shoulder.

"Don't worry. I know a foolproof method. Hold your ears." He summoned a great breath and roared, "Forget it! I'm taking her to Pizza Hut!"

Blessed silence descended once more.

"Pizza Hut?" Domenic's grandmother quavered into the quiet. She rested her hand over her heart. "Oh, Domenic, you wouldn't."

"We've boycotted Pizza Hut for ten years," he explained to Lynne while maintaining a fierce glower to keep everyone quiet. "Grandmama swears one of their big shots must have tasted her breadsticks somewhere and stole her recipe."

"They did," Grandmama said, "but they got the Parmesan wrong."

"Grandmama, Pizza Hut did not steal your recipe."

"What does your girlfriend think?" The bosom of Grandmama's black wool dress swelled with agitation.

"She's not my girlfriend."

"It's possible." Lynne nodded thoughtfully.

"Huh?"

"Corporations do steal, Domenic. It's not a pretty fact, but it's true."

Grandmama straightened her narrow shoulders, and her disapproving frown melted briefly into a smug see-I-told-you-so expression.

Not even Domenic's sisters put any credence in Grandmama's breadstick claims, and here was Lynne, who didn't fit at all into his family, standing up for her. He hadn't seen Grandmama smile like that since before his father died. He wished he hadn't dropped his hold on Lynne's shoulder because he felt the silly need to hug her, but that would only set back the progress he'd made in bringing his family into some semblance of quiet.

"Okay," he said, before the uproar could recommence. "Listen up, because I only want to say this once. Lynne and I are just friends." Someone snickered, and Dom shot a glare toward his brothers. "We're not getting married. We just filled out that marriage application for a chance to win tickets to the Steelers game."

Lynne nodded with so much earnest vigor that it deflated his ego just a little.

"That's not nice, Domenic," his mother reproached. "You men are all alike, letting football interfere with your marriage."

"It's not going to interfere, because there's not going to be a marriage."

His mother merely sniffed, and then she put her arm around Lynne's shoulders. "I don't blame you, honey. Men and their football. Give me your coat. I'll fix you a nice dish of pasta. I made special meatballs. Let him go to Pizza Hut by himself and watch football on the television."

Great. Now his family turned against him while embracing Lynne to their literal bosom. There wasn't even any football on television until the weekend.

His disgruntled amusement dissipated when he noticed the agony welling in Lynne's eyes, as if she really believed his mother would allow him to walk out the door and eat alone in a restaurant.

"Can he stay?" Lynne asked in a thready whisper.

"Only if he behaves," Mama said.

The familiar familial babble resumed. Lynne sent him a triumphant smile over her shoulder while his mother steered her toward the kitchen. Two women could not be more dissimilar, he thought, comparing his mother's comfortable, sturdy form to Lynne's stylish slenderness. Judging by the way her waist curved, she managed to squeeze a good many hours of aerobics into her busy schedule. The image of Lynne bouncing up and down while encased in spandex stimulated a hunger that had nothing to do with Grandmama's breadsticks, but quite a lot to do with Lynne's request to keep him there at her side.

The kids started dive-bombing his legs again. His brother cracked open a beer and handed it to him, and someone else turned on the hockey game. Dom craned his neck to get a good look into the kitchen and saw Lynne staring down in bafflement at a cheese grater. Something warm and fine stirred near his heart.

It felt good to be home again.

The women wouldn't allow Lynne to help with the dishes. "No, no, you're our guest," Maria Corso said, keeping Lynne in her chair with one firm hand atop her shoulder.

She couldn't very well protest, considering her sole purpose in being there was to convince the Corso clan that she truly didn't fit in, that she was a temporary, one-time-only guest. So she sat alone at the dining room table while the women made quick work of cleaning up in a manner that showed how often they must have done it together. They laughed a lot, and snapped towels at one another like the girls sometimes did at summer camp. Maybe housekeeping chores weren't as tedious when shared with others.

Over in the living room, the men lounged about, supposedly watching the kids, but paying more attention to the hockey game on television. Domenic had claimed a reclining chair a few feet away from her, near the opening between the dining room and living room. He lay back with a beer clutched in one hand, watching the game through half-lowered eyes.

Every once in a while someone would crouch down next to his chair and ask his opinion on something. From time to time, one of the women in the kitchen would holler out and ask him what he thought of the pasta, or if he had any good ideas for the upcoming summer's vegetable garden. The whole family seemed to revolve around him, just like in the old *Godfather* movie.

Oops. That was definitely a hedgehog-based comment. She hadn't noticed until Domenic pointed out her tendency to curl in on herself when she felt envious. Well, maybe she did feel just the teensiest bit envious of the way everyone totally doted on Domenic. She'd have done anything, promised anything, if she could have felt even one iota as well loved as Domenic so obviously was.

She gave herself a mental shake. She was twenty-seven years old, for heaven's sake, well past the age when she should be worried about gaining her parents' approval. She seldom dwelled so much on that uncomfortable, uneasy relationship. Finding herself so immersed in a family who embodied everything she'd ever longed for must have triggered those old hurts.

She ought to leave. Find her coat and purse and excuse herself, get home and put in a couple of hours on her presentation for next week's planning session. But it felt so good to sit there, with her belly filled with the best meal she'd eaten in months, watching Domenic and his family.

A small brown-haired, brown-eyed boy—Lynne thought someone had called him Joey—climbed into the chair next to her and knelt there, staring unblinkingly at her.

"Hi," she said. He didn't answer. His mother had probably taught him not to talk to strangers. She certainly didn't want to interfere with any parental strictures, so she drew back from him. The kid's eyes widened with alarm, and then he bolted from the chair and dove straight into Domenic's midsection.

"Ow, Uncle Dom! Your stomach's too hard."

"Then go jump on your dad for a while. He's got a nice, soft beer belly." But as he said the words, Domenic's arm curled around the child, who snuggled back against him trustingly.

The child glanced back at Lynne. He cupped his hand and whispered ostentatiously toward Domenic's ear. "How come she looks so pretty sometimes and so mean sometimes?"

Joey's comment made Lynne draw back even more.

She'd said exactly one word to the child, which he'd ignored, and he was calling *her* mean? "I'm not mean," she muttered to herself.

The child nodded solemnly. "You look mean *right now.*"

"Nah." Domenic's hand tousled Joey's hair. "She just puts on her business face sometimes so nobody can tell what a big softy she is deep down inside."

"I don't have a business face."

"Sure you do. Like this, right Joey?" Domenic pursed his lips and sucked in his cheeks; he arched both brows until his forehead almost disappeared, and then he tilted his nose toward the ceiling. The child shrieked with laughter and then screwed his features into an imitation of Domenic's expression.

"I don't look like that," Lynne whispered.

"Sometimes."

"She's doing it again, Uncle Dom! Fix it for her." Joey squirmed off of Domenic's lap and rushed over to pat Lynne's knee. "Don't worry. Uncle Dom can fix everything. C'mon, Uncle Dom. Fix her face."

Domenic shrugged with an apologetic little smile. He left his chair and crouched easily next to her, bringing his face level with hers. She could put her hands on his shoulders if she wanted, and feel the slide of his shirt against the smooth bulge of his shoulders. Or maybe she could drift her fingers through the silky curls peeking out through the open vee of his shirt. Or maybe . . . or maybe she should sit on her hands until she got over these ridiculous impulses.

Domenic rested his fingertip near the corner of first one eye and then the other. "I'll just tip these up a little bit." His finger stroked down her cheek and came to rest at the edge of her lips. "She has to remember to keep these tilted up too." His finger skimmed over her lips to the other edge. "Both sides. Instant smile, no more business face."

A chorus of hoots and wolf whistles erupted from the male side of the room, and she sent a fervent thanks heavenward that she hadn't indulged in touching him. "Hands off, Dom," one of his brothers called. "There's nothing going on between you two." The women spun around to see what the commotion was all about and caught Domenic's finger resting on her lips. Grandmama Corso nudged Domenic's mother; they both smirked.

"Okay, okay." Domenic lifted his hand away and held it over his head in a gesture of surrender.

Lynne fought the urge to press his fingers back to her lips, to remind him that a hands-on kind of guy shouldn't suddenly adopt a hands-off attitude. She told herself that the pounding of her heart came from being so suddenly thrust into the center of attention.

Little Joey, oblivious to the room's undercurrents, stood studying her face with a critical eye. "Her nose still sticks up in the air."

"I like it like that," said Dom, rousing a spark of warmth in Lynne's heart. "You want women with noses that point upward, Joey, because it means they're smart and strong and maybe a little bit stubborn and won't take any crap from anybody."

"None of your other girlfriends had noses that pointed up, Uncle Dom."

"Lynne's not my girlfriend."

"Okay, then I'll take her. But no more business face," the child admonished Lynne.

Right then, with the memory of Domenic's touch tingling against her skin, creating smiles for her, she didn't think she'd ever be able to revert to that business face again.

Lynne double-checked the lock on her car door and glanced over to where Domenic leaned against his own vehicle. "You really didn't have to follow me home," she said, pretty much repeating the protest she'd made earlier.

He shrugged. "It's not very far out of my way. Besides, it's late."

She shrugged too. They were great at shrugging at each other. A sort of nonverbal communication to keep reminding each other that they had nothing in common, nothing important between them. "I often work this late."

"I'm sorry."

She bristled a little. She hoped he wasn't standing there feeling sorry for her because she worked hard and came home alone to an empty condo. But then a man who melded so effortlessly into the hordes of family they'd just left, who sat there contentedly while children crawled over his lap and tugged at his hair and complained about the hardness of his stomach muscles, would probably find her quiet sanctuary of a home more like solitary confinement.

"What I meant is," he said, jumping into her silence, "I'm sorry that the evening dragged on so long. I know you didn't count on staying so late."

"Oh, I had a good time. I didn't even notice the time." She realized with a start that she'd just told him the truth. Once the women had finished with the dishes, all the adults had gathered around the massive dining room table for several hours of joking and laughing. She'd been so caught up in it all that she'd never given the passage of time a single thought. "I thought you were apologizing for following me home."

"You know guys. We do stuff like this to mollify our caveman instincts."

She'd spent the whole of the drive alternately fretting over whether his following her meant he expected to be invited into her home, and knowing she wouldn't mind too much if that's what he intended. Now she knew he'd anticipated nothing; he was just obeying some instinctive male impulse. Those impulses must just come naturally to such a broad-shouldered guy. She couldn't help sneaking a peek at those shoulders, and couldn't help thinking how nice it would feel to curl up against him the way little Joey had done, to feel those big, strong arms of his wrap around her and let her know he liked her exactly the way she was.

The wind parted his open jacket, smoothing his shirt against his stomach, that hard stomach his nieces and nephews had delighted in pounding, and coffee definitely seemed like a dumb idea. He'd sense the quiet and emptiness of her apartment, for one. And for the other, well, they'd spent most of the evening assuring everyone that they had no interest in each other. Coffee would be crossing a line.

She would never see him again after tonight, unless they won the tickets.

But coffee, even decaffeinated, still crossed a line.

"They liked you," Domenic said.

"I liked them too," she said, meaning it.

"They can be overwhelming en masse. You handled yourself really well."

"Thanks."

"Well." He lifted himself away from the car, and she forcibly shifted her thoughts away from wondering at the byplay of muscle and sinew required to make the motion. It had been a long time since she'd touched a man, which was probably why she found herself so fascinated at the notion of running her hands along Domenic's abdomen to gauge the hardness of his muscles for herself.

No way was she inviting him up for coffee.

He didn't seem interested anyway. "I'll just stick around until you get in the front door."

"You don't have to . . ." she began, but she could see by the cavemanlike tightening of his jaw that he meant to watch over her anyway. "Well, thanks, then. And good night."

"Good night."

The tapping of her heels always echoed from the walls lining the parking lot, but tonight the sound was muted, as if Domenic's large, solid presence absorbed some of the solitary sound. She dealt with the door lock and glanced over her shoulder to smile an additional good-bye.

"Lynne?" he called.

"Yes?" Her heart pounded. If he asked her, point-blank, to invite him in, she would . . . she would . . .

Oh, God, she would.

"You're a good sport."

She had to blink away the ridiculous disappointment that surged through her.

"That's me," she quipped. "Lynne Stanford, good sport."

She locked the door behind her and stood in the hallway, listening, while the sounds of his car receded into the distance.

SEVEN

Dom cupped a hand over his ear, struggling to hear over the mall noises while June rattled off the list of messages she claimed couldn't wait for his return to the office.

"That's all?" he asked, disappointed that all the calls were work related. But then, what else could he expect when checking his office messages? His family was pretty good about limiting their calls during working hours. And he never gave his office number to women he dated. Except for Lynne. And he didn't really date Lynne.

He hadn't talked to her since saying good night outside her condo. Not that he was counting the hours or anything.

Or maybe he was. She'd said something about the ticket lottery being held today, Wednesday. That's probably what he had on his mind—Steelers tickets. Not Lynne Stanford.

"Well, there is one more message." There was a definitely snotty edge in June's voice. "Lynne Stanford called."

"Why didn't you say something sooner?" he demanded.

"You said you only wanted to hear the important messages. And you very emphatically told me there was nothing important going on between you two."

June no doubt still smarted from his refusal to give her the juicy details about his relationship. She didn't believe there were no juicy details. He'd pay her back later, once this little surge of elation cleared and he had a clear head to plot his revenge.

"Did she say anything about me?" He winced as soon as he'd asked the question. He should have waited for that clear head before sounding off like a teenager, asking an intermediary to interpret the comments of a girl he kind of liked.

To her credit, June didn't gloat or rub it in. "I'll quote her exactly: 'We won.' "

He let out a whoop that drew the startled regard of the bustling mall patrons. Mike, busy jotting notes onto his clipboard, looked over in surprise. Dom sent him a thumbs-up.

"Dom," said June, "did you hear what I said about the McAllister bid? They're anxious to hear from you."

"Uh, yeah," Dom lied, not recalling a word about the McAllister conversation. "I'll handle it when I get into the office. Later."

He cut off the call right in the middle of June's disbelieving sniff.

"What's up, boss?" Mike asked.

"I got tickets for the play-off game on Sunday."

"All right!" Mike stuck out his hand for a congratulatory shake.

"With Lynne," Dom added, liking the way it sounded.

"Lynne? That goofy scheme with the lady suit worked?"

"Yeah." Dom grinned. Lynne Stanford, with her specification sheets and to-do lists and pulled back hair and impeccably fitted business suits had gotten him to the play-off game.

"She'll look like a thorn among roses if she wears one of them suits to the game," Mike said.

"She's a fan. She'll wear jeans." Tight ones, Dom hoped. "Steeler shirt." Nice and loose, to give her bouncing room when she jumped. He swallowed, and his thumb raced over the cell phone pad as he started punching in Lynne's number.

"I thought you just talked to June," Mike said.

"I'm calling Lynne."

"Without looking up her number?"

Dom's thumb hovered over the last digit. No wonder Mike had that boggle-eyed look on his face. Dom was lousy with phone numbers; he couldn't even remember his own cell phone number for God's sake. And yet here he was dialing up Lynne for the first time ever with as much familiarity as if he'd actually called her a thousand times, instead of just *thinking* of calling her, which he'd done pretty much nonstop since he'd last seen her.

This was not a good sign.

Dom swiveled his thumb and depressed the "end" button.

"It's no big deal, remembering her phone number," he said.

"Heck no," Mike said, far too cheerfully. "There comes a time in every man's life when he starts committing phone numbers to memory. Next thing you know, your brain'll be sneaking around behind your back, memorizing the phone number of everyone you meet, not just the one woman you're not interested in."

"Yeah," Dom said uncertainly.

"And before you know it, you'll trim a complete set of letters of the alphabet, to go along with that letter *L* you carved in McCarry Steel's holly bush this morning."

Domenic had hoped Mike hadn't noticed that little lapse on his part. "I was thinking about the Lynch Park Mall bid," he lied. "Get it—*L* for Lynch."

"Yeah. *L* for Lynne . . . ch." Mike turned the name into two syllables having no mall relation at all.

"How 'bout them Steelers?" Dom settled for trying to change the subject.

"I don't care what you say. A tiger lily can't change its stripes. She'll probably wear sensible heels and a business suit to the game," Mike said.

Then Dom would never know if she bounced.

But she sure could smile. He rubbed his thumb surreptitiously against his fingertips, remembering the way her lips had felt when he'd fixed her business face, so soft and trembling as they'd curved in response to his touch. The way her eyes had tilted at the edges and flared with a heat that she seemed afraid to let loose.

Probably because she didn't have "get sexy" penciled in on her to-do list yet.

But oh, man, wouldn't he like to be around when she let that item reach the top of her list.

"Are you sure this lady's wrong for you, Dom?"

"No doubt about it." He deliberately quelled how right it had felt to touch her. "You know what she did? She refused to hold my little niece last night when I took her to meet my family. There's no way a refuser of babies fits into my family."

"Right." Mike frowned. "It's funny you should mention that, though. My sister told me once that she wished strangers would stop grabbing at her baby, on account of the little kid gets scared when somebody he doesn't know tries to pick him up. Poor little guy turns all red and yells so hard, she's afraid he'll burst a blood vessel or something."

Sort of the way his niece had reacted when she'd been shoved at Lynne.

He wished suddenly that he and Mike had brought work tools to the job instead of clipboards for taking notes on what needed to be ordered for the upcoming Easter displays. He had the urge to sink his hands deep into the dirt and start tearing things out by the roots.

"You know," he said, "that areca palm over near the stairs looks way too sullen and confident."

Mike peered toward the areca. "It's a tree, boss. Trees can't afford to act sullen. They're doomed by nature to be content."

"It probably thinks it can't be replaced, just because it's sent down deep roots."

"Oh well, roots, sure. Roots inspire confidence. No matter how you tear at them, there's always a few little strands left, ready to sprout back up. Tough to grub out roots, even when they're hanging on where they don't belong. What do you have against that tree anyway?"

"It's crowding out the other plants." Domenic glared at the tree, imagining the twisted tangle of roots twining beneath the surface, hanging on at the expense of the rest of the garden. Sort of the way ideas got into a man's head and planted themselves so deep that even when he suspected they might be wrong, he had a hell of a time getting rid of them. Ideas like maybe the right woman for him had to be a happy homemaker just like his mother and sisters. He'd been bringing home women like that for the past ten years without ever feeling the sense of pride and rightness he'd had with Lynne sitting next to him at the dinner table.

He wanted to call her, hear her smooth, sultry voice tell him that they'd taken a chance and won, hear her laugh with genuine happiness, hear the wondering pride in her voice when she crowed over taking a risk that had paid off for her. She liked to push herself into places where she didn't belong. He wanted to hear her make some smart remark telling him that his old-fashioned notions were full of hot air and that she'd decided to show him that he was all wrong in thinking they could never make it together.

But she wasn't available to talk to him.

She wasn't available the next three times he tried, either, and so he had to settle for leaving a message with her secretary.

He didn't have time to call a woman more than four times, especially when she obviously had no time to talk to him.

They passed the areca palm on the way out to the truck.

"*Hasta la vista*, baby." Mike gave the tree a mock salute.

"I'm keeping it," said Dom.

"But—"

"It stays. Taking it out would cause too much disruption to the rest of the garden."

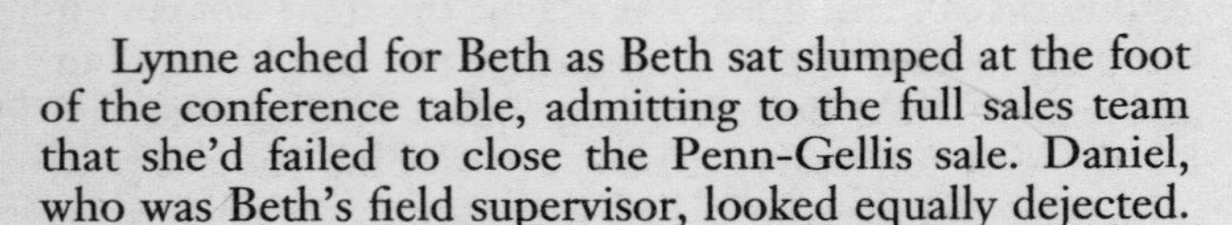

Lynne ached for Beth as Beth sat slumped at the foot of the conference table, admitting to the full sales team that she'd failed to close the Penn-Gellis sale. Daniel, who was Beth's field supervisor, looked equally dejected.

They looked the way she'd felt the other morning, when Susan had shattered her hopes. But today, a glimmer of confidence curled through her. She could close that Penn-Gellis sale. She knew she could. The old familiar excitement surged through her veins. She couldn't remember how many meetings she'd sat through lately, pretending disinterest when talk turned to sales strategy, when she really wanted to jump in. Funny, how she'd let herself forget how much she enjoyed the thrill of the chase, until she'd admitted her preference to Domenic.

But she couldn't afford to step on Daniel's or Beth's toes.

"Okay, we've been in this meeting too long. What's next on the agenda?" Susan asked.

"Could we stay on Penn-Gellis for just a minute more?" Lynne asked.

They all reacted as if their chairs had suddenly zapped them with electric shocks. Lynne felt a little brain-fried herself. Something must have happened to her mental circuits—she *never* spoke out at meetings without having a well-prepared plan in reserve. She couldn't believe she'd opened her big mouth. The prudent thing to do was simply back off. But Susan stared at her expectantly, Daniel with wariness. Lynne wished she knew how to silently convince him that she wasn't out to make him look incompetent—but realized she'd seldom smiled at Daniel. He was competition, after all, when it came to promotions, and one of the Stanford commandments said *Thou shalt not share secrets if it makes someone else look good.*

"I worked on the Penn-Gellis account when I first joined the company," she said. "I just wanted to tell Daniel and Beth that they're welcome to my old files. There might be something there that could help."

Daniel's eyes flashed with surprise—and gratitude. "At this point, anything will be appreciated. I'm not ready to give up on that account yet. I don't suppose you have any great ideas to go along with those files?"

She'd taken a risk, and he'd met her halfway. She gave him a smile and a short, quick nod.

Susan's mouth formed a pleased little *O.* "Okay, you three are a team on this now. Do what it takes."

Lynne could barely contain her elation later as she walked back to her desk. She could smell coffee brewing. Chocolate-almond-coconut coffee. The Steelers were in the play-offs, and she was going. She had a chance to go back into the field for a significant sale. She picked up her messages, feeling another surge of well-being when she leafed through them and saw that Domenic had called.

Life was good.

"This has been some day," she said when Domenic answered his office telephone.

"Yeah. I heard we won the tickets." He sounded bored, as if she were a nuisance telephone solicitor who'd interrupted his dinner to tell him he might have already won a valuable prize. Her great mood deflated a little, and she realized just how much she'd been looking forward to talking to him. She'd imagined he would be as excited as she'd felt upon hearing they'd won. Instead, he sounded brisk, no-nonsense . . . sort of the way she usually sounded on the telephone.

She wanted to tell him how his forcing her to acknowledge how much she missed selling had given her the impetus to speak up in the conference room. She'd imagined his voice warm with approval, his eyes glowing with delight, and the smile lines curving the edges of his lips and crinkling the skin around his eyes. She wanted that Domenic, not this cold and disinterested stranger.

"So what's the next step?" he asked.

She sat back in her chair, puzzled by his distance. His brusqueness reminded her that she was busy, too, much too busy to be worrying about a man's moods. She tamped down the urge to ask him what was wrong. She pulled her day planner into the center of her desk. She checked her afternoon schedule again, even though she'd already gone over it twice and knew squeezing the necessary time out of it would be really tough. "They don't want to send the tickets through the mail. Actually, the clerk was kind of adamant about both of us showing up at four o'clock. She said her boss is very keen to meet us."

She heard the rustle of papers and imagined he must be leafing through his organizer. "Four's good. We'll go together."

Together. Maybe she'd imagined his distance. She felt a little shiver of anticipation that came from more than just the thought of actually holding her very own play-off ticket in her hands.

"June didn't think you could make it."

"June doesn't know how to prioritize nearly as well as she thinks she does," he ground out.

June had been perhaps a little indiscreet in telling Lynne a great deal about Domenic's hectic afternoon schedule. So she knew he was lying. It would take some major reshuffling on his part to meet her. He prioritized meeting her higher than the McAllister bid, which June had hinted was extremely important. She glanced down at her calendar and then at her watch. Now that she looked at it again, she found it was possible to do a little creative shuffling of her own. She was just about to tell him that four o'clock would be fine when he stopped her.

"It's not that I don't trust you to hand over my ticket," he said.

"I never thought that." Now she knew why he was so willing to put himself out to meet her. He was afraid she'd waltz off with both tickets.

"The crowds will be terrible on Sunday. I don't think we should try meeting outside the stadium, that's all."

"Oh, absolutely. I agree absolutely."

"Yeah, well." He sounded unhappy, but since he'd started the conversation on that note, she couldn't even take any consolation from thinking that he might have realized that he'd insulted her integrity. "And don't forget—that clerk hinted the first time we were there that her boss wouldn't like hearing that the winners aren't really romantically involved."

"I remember," she said.

"We'll have to pretend we're for real."

"It . . . it'll just be for a few minutes." She swallowed against the hurt swelling near her heart. "No sweat."

"I'll pick you up at three forty-five."

"No, that's okay." She closed her eyes. He was trying to fix everything, work out all the details, that's all. He didn't really want to see her. "I'll meet you at the courthouse at four."

"Fine. I'll call and tell them we'll be there."

She eased her phone into the cradle, fighting the ridiculous urge to cry.

EIGHT

"So, here we are again," Domenic said as he settled into the chair beside Lynne.

She nodded, too distracted to speak. He must have showered right before coming to meet her. His hair clung to the back of his neck in barely damp tendrils while a clean, soapy scent wafted from him, overriding the stale paper smells of the office. She forced herself to breathe normally with the stern reminder that she didn't have time to waste catching up on her breath later. Nor did she have time to keep coming back to a marriage license bureau with a man she would never marry.

"The Steelers better win," she said. "These tickets cost us a fortune, if you break it down on an hourly basis."

He gave her an odd look. "Yeah, I guess so. If you look at it that way."

She always looked at things that way, but his observation made her wonder how often she'd done that in the past, complaining about her precious time being wasted without regard for the other person's feelings. She'd sounded like she grudged every minute she spent in his company. She didn't, not exactly. She grudged the wasted time, but then it wasn't exactly wasted when she was with him . . .

Her convoluted thinking made her head spin. Those short circuits in her brain seemed to be worsening rather than improving, at least when she was within range of Domenic Corso and his high-voltage distractions. She put her hand to her forehead and so didn't notice at first that their benefactor had come out into the waiting area.

Domenic leaped to his feet so eagerly that she knew he'd been waiting for an excuse to move away from her.

"Well, well, well. I'm Marvin Kane, Register of Wills."

"Register of Wills?" Lynne asked.

"My office is the height of efficiency, Ms. Stanford," Kane said. "Some people consider marriage a death sentence, so we can take care of them coming and going, right?"

The clerk sent them a thin, strained smile that said she'd heard versions of the quip more than a few times before.

Kane checked his watch and then glanced at the wall clock. He took Domenic's hand and began pumping it with enthusiasm. "Let me be one of the first to congratulate you and the little lady."

Little lady? Lynne immediately lost all guilt over accepting the tickets under false pretenses. She was on the verge of informing him that she was no little lady when Domenic caught her hand and pulled her up beside him. He stood a good head taller than she, which made objecting to being called little seem moot, but yet standing next to Domenic, with his hand holding hers, she felt more like an equal partner. That made no sense, though, because Domenic was the type of guy who really *was* interested in little ladies.

They exchanged polite comments, and then Kane handed Lynne a ticket envelope. "Guard these with your life," he admonished.

Accepting the tickets reminded her that the only reason they were standing there side by side was because Domenic hadn't trusted her. She tucked them into her purse, sending Domenic a slanting look. His eyes followed those tickets the way a hungry dog watches its master's fork move from plate to mouth. Well, he could sit up and beg, but it wouldn't do him a bit of good. He'd just have to trust her until they got outside. It would look awfully suspicious if she split up the tickets now.

Marvin Kane checked his watch against the wall clock again. It really was an annoying habit he had there. He cleared his throat. "It's four-thirteen. It'll take you two minutes to get outside. You'd better get going if you want to miss the mass exodus. Most of the courthouse offices close at four-thirty. You can beat the traffic if you leave now."

"Thanks," said Domenic. "We wouldn't want to waste any more time."

The corridors echoed but the swooshing of elevators and conversation drifting from the upper floors hinted at the exit rush about to begin. "We'd better get moving," Lynne said.

"Sure. Where's my ticket?"

She kept walking at a fast clip while rummaging in her purse. She handed him a single ticket just as they reached the revolving door. "See you Sunday," she said, slipping into the slowly twirling pie-shaped cubicle.

Something was blinding her eyesight, so she almost ran down the man holding a video camera, who stood right outside the door. She tried to back away, but the door disgorged Domenic just then and all his hard stomach muscles pushed her from behind. His hands caught her elbows in a reflexive, steadying grip.

The cameraman staggered a little but kept his arm clamped around his expensive video camera. "Here they are," he called. "Right on schedule." Three microphones, each bearing the call letters of local TV stations, bloomed in front of their faces.

"Damn that Marvin Kane," Domenic muttered. He spoke close to her ear. The low rumble shot straight through her, making her all too aware of how their bodies were pressed together.

Though half-blinded by a series of camera flashes, Lynne could see a second cameraman filming a blond news reporter as she spoke earnestly into her microphone. The clamor of questions being thrown at her deadened Lynne's ability to hear, but by the way the reporter gestured toward the courthouse entrance, Lynne knew that she was talking about *them.*

Oh, hell.

"When's the wedding date?"

"How did you two meet?"

"How long have you been engaged?"

"No comment," Lynne said.

"Hey, we're not asking you to confess to murder," protested one of the reporters.

Just then Lynne *was* feeling kind of like a criminal. She could just see it now, head shots of herself and Domenic on *America's Most Wanted*, accompanied by the slug saying they'd applied for their marriage license under false pretenses.

"Don't pick on her," Dom said. "She knows how shy I am. She's trying to protect me."

That got them laughing. And it started a warm glow in Lynne's heart. Domenic was trying to protect her—not that she needed it. Lynne heard the whup-whup-whup of the revolving door behind her, and then Marvin Kane's falsely surprised voice asking, "Well, well, well. What's this?"

Everything clicked into place as Kane posed for the cameras. "He's running for commissioner in the next election," Lynne said. "I should have realized he'd milk this ticket giveaway for free publicity."

"Yeah. That's why he was watching the time so closely. He called these guys in himself."

"So, what about those wedding plans?" repeated a reporter.

"They're not finalized yet," Dom said. That warm glow in Lynne's heart intensified a few notches. She'd never shared the sort of camaraderie with another person that let them sort of divine what the other was thinking, the way she and Domenic seemed able to do. If she didn't watch herself, she could get used to depending on him.

Whoa.

Domenic would love knowing she was tempted to depend on him; he might misinterpret it as an effort on her part to enter the world of little lady-dom, where he liked to find his women. But little ladies didn't earn two-level promotions into senior management by the age of twenty-seven. She couldn't afford getting used to depending on a man who wouldn't be around beyond Sunday, a man who wanted a woman so totally different from herself. She didn't dare let herself get thrown off track at this critical time.

"Lynne and I don't worry much about details," he said, effectively dousing any faint hope she had that he might understand and accept her for what she was.

"I didn't mind when you called me a good sport," said Lynne, "but I can't let you go on television and tell the world that I don't worry about details. I think this falls into the area of defending my professionalism."

The reporters oohed in mock dismay.

"I'm very careful," she said, sounding more earnest than she'd intended. God, what was wrong with her? A woman bent upon becoming more spontaneous shouldn't protest so much. Having Domenic Corso's well-toned body pressed against hers was definitely short-circuiting her thought processes again. The sooner she ended this, the better.

"I'm detail oriented too," Dom said.

One of the reporters yawned.

"Except when I'm around Lynne," he added.

The reporters perked up and shoved the microphones closer. Lynne shot him a dirty look. He sent her a phony apologetic smile. "Well, you have to admit that we've been acting a little out of character ever since we met."

"How long ago did you meet?" broke in a reporter.

"Long enough to know that our ultimate goal is totally compatible," Dom said with a straight face.

Well, that was true. They both wanted to go to the Steelers game with enough desperation that they'd walked open-eyed into this ridiculous scheme. And now look where taking chances had led her—lying on videotape in front of every local media outlet. Everyone at work would be talking about this. Oh, God, her *parents* might see this, and she still hadn't called them to explain. She hadn't talked to them in weeks, and they didn't know anything about the phony marriage license scheme.

"Give us a kiss," urged one reporter.

"You heard him—he's too shy," Lynne said.

"He doesn't look so shy to me," the blonde said, running a practiced gaze the length of Domenic's body.

Lynne wanted to punch her, but only because she was getting tired of watching other women ogle Domenic while he was at the marriage license bureau with her. There was another specification for her future husband: He shouldn't be so damned attractive to other women.

"One little kiss," cajoled the news guy from KDKA.

They all took up the clamor; even Marvin Kane, who had snagged a reporter and cameraman and trapped them in a corner where they were more or less forced to keep their camera and microphone focused on him. A few early courthouse departees had come through the doors and gathered around curiously. They took up the chant too.

"Tell them you don't want to do this," Lynne whispered up at Domenic. She just knew that kissing him would be a terrible mistake, and yet she felt a definite surge of interest to know what it would feel like. "This will probably be on television tonight. We'll set back all the progress we made with your family."

"On TV, huh?" His brow furrowed as if he hadn't done so much hard thinking in years. "How would I live it down if my buddies see that I passed on the chance to kiss a pretty girl? I think this falls into the area of defending my manhood."

He'd twisted her own words and objections to suit

himself. She tried to summon a frosty glare, but her lips seemed to have developed miniature minds of their own. They trembled, entirely too eager to kiss him.

"Make it a good one!" challenged the blonde as Domenic's hands came up to Lynne's shoulders and he spun her around.

He pulled her close. She should have buttoned her coat, she realized belatedly. But she hadn't, and since he never zipped his jacket, only a couple of layers of winterweight cloth separated them. She got to feel for herself how hard those stomach muscles were when they came up against her own. How firm his chest felt against her breasts, how rock-solid his thighs against hers.

"Fake it," she whispered.

"What?"

"Just a little peck. Disinterested. So people will know we're doing it because we have to, not because we want to kiss each other."

He chuckled, a low, heated rumble that passed from him straight through her. "Not a chance. Pucker up." A smile curved his lips as he lowered them to hers. Her first and only kiss from Domenic Corso would always and forever be associated with warmth and delighted laughter in her mind.

Once she got her mind back.

Her mind, her sense, her certainty that this man was utterly wrong for her, all deserted her the second his lips touched hers. This had never ever happened to her before. She knew he was a big man, but she hadn't realized just how big until she found it necessary to grab on to him for support because her knees suddenly forgot how to stay locked. His lips stroked over hers, so warm and far softer than any man with such hard stomach muscles should have. They were firm, demanding, and she knew that this brief kiss only offered a hint of what Domenic could do with his lips and tongue.

Her mind jolted back to reality with that thought. She pushed herself away from him but somehow the kiss held. Their lips parted long, long after six inches of frigid winter air separated their bodies.

Lynne stood there swaying, shuddering with the knowledge of how right she'd been in thinking that kissing Domenic would lead to disaster. Kisses that good led a woman into mooning her way through the day and planning sexy nights involving bath oil and silk sheets. She didn't have time for bath oil and silk sheets. She didn't have time for mooning.

Domenic stared down at her, frowning a little, and she wondered if her eyes looked as troubled and confused as his.

"Hey, thanks!" called one of the reporters. Lynne finally mustered a cool, unaffected smile, and turned to tell them something equally cool and unaffected, but they were gone. Just like that.

Domenic had jammed his hands into his pockets and turned to stare unblinkingly past the thickening rush-hour traffic.

She wanted to rest her hand against his biceps. She wanted to lean into the warmth of his unzipped jacket. She wanted to kiss him again.

Terror rocked through her at the realization. She had to flee from those treacherous impulses that seduced her with whispers that maybe it was time to indulge in some postponed pleasures.

"We can't do this," Lynne said.

"Do what?"

"We have to give those tickets back. They should go to someone who really wants to get married."

"Are you nuts? I'm not giving back my ticket."

"We have to. We were wrong to do this. Dishonest."

His eyes narrowed. "You knew going into this that we weren't being honest. And you know we aren't the only couple who fudged applying for a license to get the chance to win those tickets. You're not having an attack of conscience now, Lynne."

"Oh? Then what would you call it?"

"You're morphing into a hedgehog right in front of my eyes."

"I didn't say anything nasty," she countered.

"Not this time—but you're curling up and trying to hide. You're split right down the middle, Lynne. You're a tiger when it comes to proving how strong and independent you are. But the minute you begin to feel soft and close to someone, you flash the bristles. Kissing me wasn't on your to-do list. Liking it sure as hell isn't on your agenda, so you're backing off."

"I'm not backing off."

"The hell you're not." He stuck out his upper teeth and made tiny, quick little biting motions against his lower lip. "Hedgehog."

"You look like a woodchuck," she said, ridiculously, tearfully furious. "Hedgehogs are much cuter than that."

"Nobody cares how cute they are if you get stabbed every time you touch one."

"I didn't stab you. I kissed you."

"And it was so good that it scared you, and now you're trying to run away."

"It wasn't *that* good," she lied. And then she caught her breath. She'd really done it now. Let her emotions goad her into speaking without thinking, flinging out something hurtful to deflect him away. She couldn't even apologize, because then she'd have to admit that the kiss had been terrific.

She waited for him to call her on it. Instead, he just shifted position, placing distance between his warm, solid body and hers.

Her throat tightened. That leaden sensation squeezed her chest.

"We can't give those tickets back right now anyway," Dom said in enviably even tones. He nodded toward the revolving doors, whipping ceaselessly with a steady stream of departing courthouse workers. He was right about that too. Even if they managed to buck the outgoing tide, the marriage license bureau was sure to be closed by now.

"Tomorrow," Lynne forced through her lips. "I'm busy all morning, but I can take the tickets back late in the afternoon."

He studied her for a long moment. He looked very unhappy, and she felt a rush of guilt. She'd conned him into this scheme and now that they'd won, she was trying to deny him the reward he'd earned. And all because when he'd kissed her, she'd forgotten herself for a moment. Forgotten herself. A woman ought to treasure kisses capable of doing that. Instead, it had scared her to death.

"I'll make you a deal," he said eventually. "Let's both think about this overnight. I'll stop by your office sometime tomorrow morning, and if you still feel the same, I'll agree to return the tickets."

"You will?" Her heart pounded. She knew how much

those tickets meant to him. She didn't think any man had ever made such a grand gesture for her.

"I want to go to the game, but not if I have to force you into going with me."

He made her feel small, petty, and a coward. All because of a kiss that she hadn't been able to handle.

"Thank you," she whispered.

"Don't thank me yet." He frowned sternly at her. "You have to promise to think about this overnight. And you'll have to bring the tickets back all by yourself—I have to go to Erie tomorrow. You'll have to admit the truth, and it might not be pleasant."

"That's only fair."

He looked even more unhappy, as if he was disappointed that she was willing to single-handedly shoulder the burden of admitting their deceit. Most guys she knew would eagerly pass along the unpleasant chore.

"I have to get back to work," she said.

"It's almost five o'clock."

"I usually work until seven or eight."

"Oh. Well, have fun."

Fun.

When she got to her car, though, she didn't feel like going back to work. She drove home instead, and let herself into the echoing quiet of her condo. The cleaning service had been there earlier in the day. The gray-frost carpets bore the lines of vacuuming. The alabaster-and-onyx carvings gleamed softly atop shining glass surfaces. Black-and-white geometric-patterned pillows lay plumped against softly burnished vanilla leather sofas. Everything was in place, but something seemed out of kilter.

She didn't have her briefcase with her.

An odd feeling, something like panic, welled up inside her. She had nothing to do. She scrambled for her keys, intending to make a quick run to the office to pick up a stack of paperwork, but then her fingers brushed against the ticket. She'd promised Domenic that she would think things through before insisting they return it.

She found a legal-size tablet and started a list of the pros and cons of returning that ticket.

She forgot to turn on the Home Shopping Network.

She labored over the list for hours, and only summoned one listing under the "pro" section:

Won't have to see Domenic ever again.

Somehow it didn't seem like such an attractive feature. She underlined the phrase once, twice, and then again, and realized she really wanted to draw a line *through* the words.

With a sigh, she turned her attention to the "con" side of the list. The disadvantages of returning the tickets flowed as effortlessly as plots from Stephen King's typewriter:

Giving those tickets back means I backed off because of one little kiss.

I'll miss the football game.

I'll prove Susan right—I don't know how to take risks and have fun.

I'll never see Domenic again . . .

Her pen paused.

How could the same phrase show up as both a pro and a con? He was right, she did split her feelings down the middle. The sensible side of her recognized him as a pure minus, a high-maintenance man who would distract her too much from her goals. The emotional side of her, the part she tried so hard to subdue, rated him a definite plus.

When she gave up and sat back to stretch her aching muscles, she saw it was almost time for the late news. She popped a blank tape into the VCR and set it to record channel eleven—they usually went in for human interest stories in a big way. She should have gone to bed, but she sat there and watched channel two's broadcast.

She'd begun to hope they'd shelved the item for more serious news when she saw it. The Kiss. Her and Domenic. If she would've blinked, she would've missed it. Impossible. That had been a Kiss with a capital *K*, and it had left her far too shaken and breathless to have lasted for only a few seconds. An earth-shattering event like that kiss deserved more than a token flash at the end of the broadcast.

They must have edited the kiss.

She switched over to channel eleven, but the news had ended. No problem. She had it on tape. She rewound, and then had to fast-forward almost the whole way through. They'd shown the kiss near the end of the broadcast, just as they'd done on the other station.

They must have edited it too. It seemed like Domenic had no sooner swooped his head down to brush her lips than it was over.

Impossible. She'd been kissed before, lots of times. But none of those kisses had roused such powerful, forceful emotions that she'd raced home without work and spent hours fabricating reasons why running from that kiss was the right thing to do.

Well, that's why VCR's had freeze-frame features. She replayed The Kiss frame by frame. She saw the clean, strong line of Domenic's jaw angle toward her.

Saw her own chin tilt up to meet him. Their lips met, clung, clung, clung. A blur at the edge of one frame soon focused into her hand, reaching up to stroke Domenic's neck, to bury her fingers in the thick, springy wealth of his hair, to draw him even closer. Oh, God, she didn't even remember doing that!

She couldn't believe she'd done that, so she rewound the tape and watched it again.

She replayed it at least twenty times.

And when she went to bed, alone, her lips tingled, her fingers ached, for the feel of him.

NINE

Where was a half-inch of snow when you needed it? The hallways echoed the solitary tapping of Lynne's heels as she hurried toward OmniCom's massive chrome-and-glass double entrance door. The day had dawned in typical Pittsburgh winter style, gloomy but dry.

So she had no convenient traffic tie-up to excuse her tardiness. She couldn't even claim that her sunglasses were perched on her nose to ward off snow blindness—the minute someone took a look at those dark circles under her eyes, they'd know she was trying to cover up the effects of a near-sleepless night. So much for the claims of that expensive eye-lift cream she'd ordered from the shopping channel. Maybe from now on, she'd try out her cosmetics at the department store counters.

She performed a quick review of the explanations she'd created for anyone who asked about The Kiss shown on yesterday's news. And then summoning a deep, fortifying breath, she pushed open the door and stepped into the bustling office. But her entrance provoked no outcry of curiosity. No demands for juicy details. A few secretaries glanced up briefly from their computers and flashed her smiles as she passed their desks, but returned to their work with deflating quickness. Beth, speaking into her telephone, gave her a distracted wave from her office, and then swiveled around so her chairback faced Lynne.

She couldn't help contrasting the general disinterest in her phony romance with the excitement that had surrounded Ellen's announcement. But back on that morning, she reminded herself, they'd all been gathered around the coffee urn with time to spare for chitchat. And they'd probably pounced on Ellen's plans because Lynne herself had been boring them by carping over the delay in getting her meeting started.

She felt suddenly, totally alone in the midst of the humming office. This was what her single-minded focus on promotion had earned her—alienation. She'd been friends with many of these people at one time, young and happy and caught up in the excitement of interesting work performed alongside interesting people. They hadn't changed, she realized. She'd been the one to withdraw from the company softball team, the one to beg off from so many ladies' nights out that they didn't bother asking her anymore, the only one to feel superior over giving up pleasure for the pursuit of promotion. There wasn't a single one of them she could have called the night before to help her work out the confusion she was experiencing. Nobody here cared about her, Lynne Stanford. Nobody here even knew the real Lynne Stanford anymore.

Lately, it seemed that she didn't even know herself.

She couldn't even remember what had been so important about that meeting the other day. But she could so easily recall the scent of chocolate-almond coffee. And her first glimpse of Domenic Corso.

Domenic. He'd promised to stop by today to see if she'd reconsidered returning the play-off tickets. Most men would've just told her forget it, they weren't giving the tickets back no matter what—but he'd promised to think about it overnight, provided she did the same. He respected her opinion, was willing to look at her side of the argument. She'd have to remember to write those qualities down on her hypothetical future husband's hypothetical specification sheet. Especially since Domenic had been right to suggest the cooling-off period. Returning the tickets wouldn't ease her mind. She'd only wonder forever after why she'd been so frightened of one tiny kiss.

"Any messages?" she asked her secretary Alyssa as she paused by her desk. Alyssa pressed a handful of pink while-you-were-out slips into Lynne's hand.

"Lynne, I have to warn you—"

Lynne read the first message. Her cousin Lisa had called? Probably because she'd seen the news. Too bad she hadn't called Lynne at home the night before, when she'd needed someone to talk to. Not that they were really close, but . . . but it had been late, and come to think of it, Lisa probably didn't have her private home phone number. And why did she have Alyssa write "catering" in on the message, as though she feared Lynne might not remember what Lisa did for a living?

"I'm expecting a visitor this morning, Alyssa," she said distractedly. "Be sure to buzz me as soon as—"

"Uh, Lynne." Alyssa grimaced. "She's here already."

"She?" Lynne drew up short.

"Your mother." Alyssa bit her lip. "I put her in your office."

"My *mother*?"

Alyssa nodded unhappily. Her shoulders drooped in a miserable slump, one which Lynne had to fight to avoid duplicating. Her mother abhorred poor posture.

"Oh, God. Alyssa, wait five minutes and then come into my office with an excuse, any excuse, to get her out of there."

"Okay. I just hope you remember this when it's time to do my performance review."

Straight-backed and grateful for the sunglasses hiding her eyes, Lynne darted into her office and slid behind the refuge of her desk.

"Mother! What an unexpected surprise."

Madeline Stanford lifted one elegantly plucked brow and glanced at her watch. "Getting in late won't endear you to your superiors, darling."

Never let your competition beat you to work in the morning. One of the thou-shalt-not-do-this business commandments, as handed down by Madeline Stanford. Lynne had memorized and incorporated every one of them. But coming in late hadn't roused an outcry; Susan hadn't rushed from her office waving a pink slip and demanding her resignation.

"I didn't sleep well last night," Lynne said, removing her sunglasses before Madeline had the chance to chide her over wearing them at her desk.

"That's evident."

While Madeline's cool gaze appraised her, Lynne ran a mental checklist to ensure she'd met all her mother's dress-for-success dictates: hair in place, jewelry expensive but tasteful, purse and shoes tooled from Italian leather, well-tailored suit. She'd bet anything that Domenic's mother would be more concerned with the dark circles under her daughter's eyes than fretting over whether or not she projected the right professional appearance.

"Well, I'm waiting," said Madeline.

"Waiting for what?"

"For some explanation of that outrageous display your father and I saw on television last night."

"You saw the news."

"One must keep up with current events, darling."

"You could have called me," Lynne said, quelling the ache that rose at knowing her mother had seen the news item and had not thought it important enough to call, had not considered that Lynne might need someone to talk to.

"You know I go to bed promptly at eleven thirty-five, darling."

Ah, yes, yet another of the Stanford success strategies: *Never go into the office looking haggard. Your boss will think you can't handle stress.* She couldn't help contrasting the things she'd learned at her mother's knee with Domenic's fond memories of sniffling back tears with his mother.

"Tell me, Mother—did we ever watch television together?"

Madeline drew back as though Lynne had slapped her, and Lynne felt a sinking disappointment. Madeline Stanford wasn't the type of woman to sit around watching sad love stories in the afternoon with her daughter. They'd never done any of the typical mother-daughter things, never created the sort of bond Lynne had always craved. And it would never change. Her mother sat right in front of her now, and Lynne still could not envision confiding in her that she'd gotten herself involved in something of a mess, that a man who was all wrong for her had kissed her and left her feeling uncertain and confused.

If she ever had a daughter, Lynne vowed, they would watch sad love stories together. They would laugh and eat chocolate and share all sorts of secrets, not just those involving corporate politics.

"Never mind." Lynne sighed. "I planned on calling you today to explain what you saw. It's not what you think."

"Oh? It seemed straightforward enough to me. The news anchor announced that my only child and a large, irresponsible-looking man had applied for a marriage license together."

"He's not irresponsible." Lynne felt a surge of outrage on Domenic's behalf.

"You're evading the real issue. We decided marriage can wait for a few years, didn't we, darling?"

"You were married and had me when you were younger than I am now." Lynne didn't understand why she was protesting instead of explaining the truth.

"Exactly. And we both know what a mistake that was. Not that I regret for a moment putting my career on hold for you." Madeline's lukewarm smile seemed to make a lie of the words. "But I thought you had learned from my experience. I certainly thought I'd taught you to choose a man who would be a social asset. Lynne, that . . . that Domenic Corso person was wearing blue jeans and a sweatshirt on television."

How dare she call him a Domenic Corso person, as if a man who preferred Levi's to Armani was some sort of subspecies of human.

"We didn't know we were going to be on television. And I happen to like the way he looks in blue jeans and sweatshirts."

She did. Although she'd blurted the admission out from anger, a sudden tingle coursed through her, remembering well-washed denim and fleece hugging Domenic's long-muscled form.

"But it doesn't matter," she quickly added. "There's nothing romantic going on between us."

"Lynne, you applied for a marriage license with the man. I'll repeat. We decided marriage could wait, didn't we?"

Lynne felt like slumping, felt like promising she'd be good, the way she always did when chided by her mother, and then righteous indignation flooded her. She was pushing thirty, for God's sake, and here she sat, allowing Madeline to lecture her like she was some precocious teenager.

"We did it as a dare, sort of. We wanted to get in on a lottery for play-off tickets."

"Play-off tickets?" Madeline looked honestly confused.

"The Steelers, Mother. Applying for the marriage license put us into a lottery for tickets to the AFC play-off game on Sunday."

"Football! I might have known." Madeline frowned down the length of her nose. "I thought you'd come to your senses about that silly sport."

"I did," Lynne said. "I made up my mind I'd get to that game somehow, and I did it."

This meeting was going badly. She didn't know what had gotten into her. Madeline Stanford was a real superwoman. Lynne had grown up admiring her chic, successful mother. She'd long since lost count of the times she'd told her mother how much she wanted to be just like her, and Madeline had reveled in her admiration, but always claimed Lynne could fly higher, achieve more, if she just profited from the wisdom gained by Madeline's mistakes. But for some reason, with Madeline sitting there looking so superior and disapproving, all Lynne could think was, *I don't want to end up like her.*

But she wouldn't be happy as a stay-at-home mom, either.

There had to be some sort of happy medium. There had to be a way for a woman to succeed at her ambitions and still revel in the joys of a family. For the first time, Lynne began to wonder whether her mother's discontent could truly be blamed on the sacrifices she'd made as a young married woman—or whether the discontent merely reflected a bitter, dissatisfied nature buried beneath a well-polished facade.

If so, she'd been emulating one doozy of a role model.

There was a discreet tap at the door frame, and Alyssa peeked in. Her eyes were wide with a hint of suppressed excitement. "Lynne, that visitor you were expecting is here."

She swung the door open, and Domenic Corso stepped into her office.

For a long, breathless moment, Lynne couldn't do anything but stare at his lips and imagine them coming at her in slow motion.

Curse all VCR's!

She cast a nervous glance at her mother, and then returned to the more agreeable task of checking out the rest of Domenic. She'd never seen anyone look less irresponsible. He had really great hair for a man, thick and springy and layered back to reveal the strong, clean lines of his face. His well-cut black suit hung just right from his broad shoulders, and his pristine white shirt contrasted against the ingrained tan of his skin. He wore a blue-and-red power tie that any business executive would covet. He looked gorgeous, impossibly elegant, and sophisticated . . . but somehow, she missed the way he looked in snug jeans and comfortable sweatshirt.

"Hi," he said, with a blindingly white flash of a grin.

"Hi," she answered faintly.

Domenic nodded toward the woman seated in one of the two chairs facing Lynne's desk and mentally kicked himself for barging in on her so early. Well, he'd warned her he would stop by before he left for Erie . . .

Who the hell was he kidding? He didn't have to be in Erie that early. But after a night of tossing and turning while his body tortured him, remembering their kiss, he simply hadn't been able to wait to see her again. "Sorry if I'm interrupting something important," he said.

"Oh, no, it's fine," said Lynne.

An uncomfortable silence gripped them all, and then the woman cleared her throat. "Lynne?"

"Oh." Lynne blushed, and she shriveled back into her chair. Every protective instinct within him surged to life. She rattled off an introduction. "Mother, this is Domenic Corso. Domenic, this is my mother, Madeline Stanford."

Her mother? The information struck him like a blow to the gut. Not because he'd dreaded the introduction, but because Lynne so obviously hated making it. She sat there looking miserable and embarrassed, and he couldn't help contrasting her reluctance to introduce them with his own quiet pride in her when he'd presented her to his family.

From the way Madeline was staring down her nose at him, Dom thought he understood Lynne's agitation. Mama Barracuda definitely did not approve.

He mentally kissed his play-off ticket good-bye.

"Domenic can't stay," Lynne said. "He's on his way to Erie for business."

"Change in plans." Perversely, her trying to get rid of him so quickly made Domenic want to hang around. Maybe Lynne was rubbing off on him. He settled into the empty chair without waiting for her invitation. "My cousin Tony called late last night and asked . . ." He slanted a glance toward Madeline and decided to wait until he had a minute alone with Lynne to propose Tony's plan. He gave a what-the-hell-can-a-guy-do kind of shrug. "The things a man'll do for his family. Erie can wait."

"Irresponsible," Madeline said through gritted teeth.

That set Domenic aback. True, he sometimes tired of being the one everyone turned to like some sort of Mr. Fix-It. But he never hesitated to set things aside when someone truly needed him, and everyone knew they could count on him. He studied Madeline and added what he observed to his insight about what made Lynne tick. The woman was polished to perfection, cold as a marble statue, and he had the sensation that he was looking upon the image of what Lynne would be like in another twenty-five years.

Physically, the two women had the same height, the same general body build, the same hair. But Madeline's eyes lacked the animation of Lynne's. He couldn't imagine their cold depths gleaming with the suppressed delight Lynne sometimes fought so hard to hide. He couldn't imagine the disapproving curve of Madeline's lips ever softening into a smile, and she had the grooves to prove that they never did.

Lynne must've learned her business face by copying her mother.

If Lynne wasn't careful, or if someone didn't come along real quick to cajole her out of it, her expression would harden into a duplicate of her mother's.

But that very obviously wasn't his concern. Lynne's reluctance to present him to her mother, her eagerness to hurry him out the door, proved that she hadn't been affected by their kiss and proved that she wasn't interested in keeping him around long enough to remind her how to smile.

He felt embarrassed suddenly, remembering how carefully he'd shaved that morning, how he'd actually used the blow-dryer instead of just raking his fingers through his hair the way he usually did. He'd dressed in his finest, sure to shock old Carlton at the decorative stone plant in Erie, who'd never seen Dom in anything but his customary jeans and sweatshirt. But he'd wanted to dress nice, and followed some macho, goofy impulse to look his best, to show her he could mingle in her world every once in a while just as easily as she'd melted into his.

"I can't believe you let him coerce you into . . . *this* . . . for a football game." Madeline practically spat the last words.

"Hey, I—" Domenic began.

And then Lynne surged to his defense. "Pull back the claws, Mother. This was my idea, not Domenic's."

It did something to him, the way she looked so frightened yet determined in facing down her mother, and he wondered if she'd ever challenged Madeline Stanford before. Probably not, judging by Madeline's reaction. She drew back, and her eyebrows rose so high, they nearly melded into the smooth line of her hair.

"*Your* idea?"

"*My* idea."

Madeline blinked, and Dom would swear she looked impressed, rather than appalled. He didn't have time to confirm the impression before Madeline attacked.

"Call it off," she ordered. "You know you can't waste time on frivolities just now."

He'd never been called a frivolity before, so it left him disinclined to point out Madeline's big mistake. Apparently Mama Barracuda didn't understand her daughter very well. Telling Lynne she couldn't have Domenic and football would only make her more determined to hold on to both. He sat back, kind of liking the way things were going.

She didn't disappoint him.

"I don't intend to do any such thing," Lynne said. "We're a team."

This morning was proving hazardous to his equilibrium. It was a new sensation for him. He'd always been the one to call the shots, to direct the flow of a relationship. Two seconds earlier he'd been convinced that Lynne had no interest in him, but now she looked at him with a soft glow lighting her eyes that made him hope she'd relived that kiss over and over the way he'd done and realized they might be on the verge of something special here. They were a team again. Domenic savored that feeling for a good, long time before he realized that he'd forgotten to be happy that she seemed willing to hold on to the play-off tickets.

"Backing out now wouldn't be very smart," Lynne said with a soft smile. "Admitting the truth could damage my career. My boss, Susan, knows the truth, and she's understanding about it, but I'd hate to have to start explaining this to everyone in senior management."

Dom's hopes deflated with the suddenness of a blown tire. There was nothing special about her soft glow; none of it had been directed toward him, it all went to her job.

He wished there was a nice solid wall close enough to bash his head into a few times, knock some sense into his thick skull. Lynne Stanford wanted one thing and one thing only from him: football tickets. The sooner he accepted that, the better off he'd be.

And he didn't know why it bothered him so much, anyway. Lynne Stanford wasn't his type. She probably couldn't wait until her face hardened into a rock-solid business face.

Madeline had paled, and Dom wondered if Lynne's remarks about damaging her career might provoke a stroke. And then he couldn't decide if Madeline was actually afraid for Lynne's career, or if she was just annoyed that she hadn't thought of the career angle before Lynne mentioned it.

Dom decided he didn't care.

"Well." Madeline stood and gathered her coat and purse. "I've done all a mother can be expected to do."

Domenic studied the hurt in Lynne's eyes, her defensive posture as she sat defiantly tall, and he wanted to say "ha!"

And then Madeline proceeded to embellish Lynne's concerns as though she'd come up with the idea herself.

"I suppose you're right, darling. Your superiors might question your judgment if they learn you entered into this scheme with such frivolous intent. However, they'll have no quarrel with you if you simply break off an inappropriate engagement at a later date. We'll do lunch one day soon and discuss how best to handle it."

"Of course." Lynne agreed with calm politeness, promising that she and her mother would meet soon to demolish all evidence that she'd ever aligned herself with Domenic Corso. Dom wondered if Lynne's quarterly meals with her father covered similar agendas.

He felt a strange tightening in his throat.

"I'm sorry about that," Lynne said after her mother had left. She lifted her hands to her forehead and massaged tiny circles near her eyebrows. When her fingers strayed toward her hairline, she stopped, as if fearing to disturb the severely pulled-back style.

"I'm sorry too," he murmured.

She looked at him, wary, daring him to pity her. He wished she hadn't done that. Pitying her would be a hell of a lot easier on his peace of mind than the grudging respect he felt. It took one strong-willed, determined fighter to stand up to a bully like Madeline Stanford, and Lynne had been fighting this battle for her whole life.

"Did you really mean what you said? You've changed your mind about returning the tickets?"

She nodded. "You were right, Domenic." His respect lost its grudging edge. She'd kept her promise and given the matter a lot of thought. "I developed a list of pros and cons and . . . well, I'd like to keep the tickets. But," she added with a severe frown, "no more kissing."

Domenic made a zipping motion across his lips and thought about what a great symbolic gesture it was, since it acceded to her demand and also served to remind himself that things like kissing were over and done between them.

He sure gave up easily, Lynne thought. He had some nerve, lecturing her on never backing up when he was so willing to wimp out at the first sign of resistance. He stuck one finger between his neck and shirt collar and tugged. The simple movement put all of him into motion, his arms flexing, his thighs bunching. Not a wimp, she amended. Maybe pushing their relationship to a higher level just wasn't a risk he was interested in taking.

This was shaping up to be one of her all-time worst days.

She tried looking on the bright side. She'd already faced her mother, so that was over with. And she knew for one-hundred-percent certain where she stood with Domenic—exactly nowhere. So there was no need for her to lose any more sleep over him. She promised herself to erase that videotape the minute she got home.

"No more kissing," Domenic repeated solemnly. "There's lots more than potentially terrific sex at stake here."

Potentially terrific sex? At once her mind plagued her with a frame-by-frame replay of their kiss, of her face tilting up to his, of their lips meeting and clinging. "Such as what?"

He tugged at his collar again, as if he'd been walloped by an erotic thought the same as she had. Or maybe he just wasn't comfortable with the tie encircling his neck. "Listen, Lynne, I came here hoping . . . well, you made it easy. I was going to beg you to stick it out with me."

"You were?" she whispered.

He leaned toward her. Her familiar office faded into

nothing more than a blurred backdrop. Domenic dominated her vision, drawing her focus as effortlessly as nectar drew a honeybee.

"I wasn't sure you'd go along. I mean, you don't know anything about me, the kinds of things that are important to me."

"You don't know anything about me, either."

His expression turned a little bleak, and then he shook his head, as if changing gears in midthought. "I practiced all the way over here, trying to find just the right words. I wasn't sure I could convince you it was worth it, but he'd really appreciate the chance."

"He? He who?" Oh, God, what had happened to her grammar? What had happened to Domenic's, referring to himself in the third person as if he were some kind of royalty?

"My cousin Tony. That's what I started to tell you while your mother was here. Tony called me last night. He runs a limo service, and business has been really lousy. He thought that if he chauffeured us back and forth from the game, we might mention his company name during one of our interviews, and he'd get some free publicity. I can't let him down."

His cousin Tony. Lynne felt the heat sneaking up her neck to her cheeks and prayed he hadn't noticed that she'd thought their conversation was headed in an entirely different direction. An unzipped-lip direction. She especially hoped he hadn't noticed how mushy and little-ladyish she'd gotten when he said he wanted her to stick with him, as if she'd been almost tempted to march in lockstep with that old Tammy Wynette song.

She couldn't understand herself. She was the one

who'd been insisting from the minute they embarked on this course that there was nothing going on between them. *She'd* declared her lips off limits. There was no reason for her to feel so god-awful disappointed that he agreed with her, no reason to want to cry because his only purpose in carrying on was to help his cousin Tony.

From somewhere she grabbed on to the few remaining strands of her pride. She smiled brightly. "What a coincidence. My cousin Lisa runs a catering business that's not doing so well. She called this morning to ask if we'd like her to cater the world's greatest pregame tailgate party in exchange for the publicity." She crossed her fingers, praying that Lisa's phone message did indeed indicate such a willingness. "I was hoping you hadn't changed your mind about the tickets, for Lisa's sake."

"I see." His throat worked, and he gave a strangled-sounding little laugh. "For Lisa."

"And Tony," she reminded him, "providing he's a good driver. I mean, if we're going to sort of endorse him."

"He used to drive trucks for a living. But now that you mention that endorsement angle—I hope your cousin Lisa brings Buffalo wings for the tailgate. I couldn't hype a caterer who didn't do wings at tailgates."

"Oh, sure, Buffalo wings are one of her specialties." Lynne endured a pang of remorse. She didn't even know what her cousin's catering company prepared, while Domenic seemed to know all the ins and outs of his cousin Tony's business. Knowing Domenic, he probably did Tony's bookkeeping for him.

"So let me make sure I have this clear. We're going to keep the tickets. For the sake of our cousins."

"Well, our cousins and that job issue I mentioned to my mother." She was suddenly grateful that she'd tossed that idea at her mother, because now it didn't sound as if she'd invented the excuse on the spur of the moment.

"Okay. Our cousins, and your career."

"That just about covers it."

"And since we're only going along with each other as sort of a good deed, we don't have to feel guilty about keeping the tickets as a reward, right?"

"No guilt."

"Well, that's great." He stood and jammed his hands in his pockets, looking as if he missed his comfortable bomber jacket. "I'd better get going if I want to make it to Erie by noon. Besides, I've probably blown a hole in your schedule."

"I can catch up tonight."

He nodded, looking somber. "I'll call you tomorrow." Her traitorous heart thundered against her breast. "I'll need your address and directions for Tony, so he can pick you up before the game."

"Great. We won't have any parking hassles."

He inclined his head toward her, and then he was gone.

Lynne went to the door and watched him move through the outer office. Every woman in the room stared after him with some mixture of awe and lust. And once he was gone, once the huge chrome-and-glass doors swung shut behind him, they turned their heads back toward her, and she could read the mingled envy and disbelief on their faces.

"There's nothing going on between us," she announced.

She stepped into her office and closed the door. She leaned back against it, shaking so hard that she didn't know how she'd calm down enough to tackle all the things on her to-do list for the day.

She'd be really, really glad when this was over.

TEN

Lynne had ridden in white limos, in black limos, but never in one that had been tiger-striped in mustard-yellow and black, with "Let's Go Steelers" pennants suction-cupped to the top of each fender as if they were diplomatic flags. Black-and-gold pompons and twisted garlands looped in elongated figure eights over the hood and trunk, and a three-foot-long Steelers banner waved from the radio antenna.

Slanted against the trunk, where a Just Married sign would ordinarily go, someone had duct-taped a hand-lettered sign: *Official Haulers of Pittsburgh's Steelers Sweethearts.*

The limo driver bounded out of the driver's seat, wearing what looked like a regulation Steelers uniform. The name CORSO was emblazoned across the back of his shirt. He wrestled off the helmet and stuck out his hand.

"Hey, Lynne. Nice to see you again."

It took Lynne a moment before she remembered

meeting him at Domenic's mother's house, but then he hadn't had helmet hair plastered down against his forehead. "Hi, Tony. Um, interesting limo."

"Ain't it?" He grinned proudly at the car. "Let's hope it don't rain, on account of that paint's temporary."

"I'll keep my fingers crossed," she promised. She hoped for his sake that the paint would wash off, that the sign could be untaped, without damaging the underlying finish.

He pointed to the tailgate sign as they passed behind the car, and then stopped dead so that she bumped into him. "I know, I know," he said with a put-upon sigh. "You're probably wondering why I left the sign's top section blank."

Lynne studied the hand-lettered sign. Corso men must be big on block printing, she thought, remembering Domenic's note seeking play-off tickets. "Oh, sure, I was wondering about that blank spot from the minute you pulled up."

"I left it blank, 'cause I been having a little bit of trouble thinking up a catchy name for my business."

He blushed a deep brick-red and looked at her expectantly.

She was about to tell him that helping businesses *after* they'd been named was more in her line of expertise, but from his fidgeting embarrassment, she knew he'd struggled over making the request. She wondered if this was the way Domenic always felt, wanting to help but not being sure he was doing the right thing.

"I've always heard that it's a good idea to pick a name that starts with the letter *A*," she ventured. "Use an *A* word, and you'll be listed first in the yellow pages."

"I heard that, too, but my competition already beat

me to it. There's ABC Limos, and A-1 Autos, all kinds of names start with *A* and a dash."

"Your name's really Anthony, right?" He nodded. "How about A-Anthony Autos?"

"A-Action would still come ahead of me," he said with a glum shake of his head. "See, this ain't as easy as you might think."

"No, it isn't." She puckered her brow, thinking. "How about if you spell Anthony with two *A*'s?" She grimaced; the idea sounded pretty lame. "On second thought, spell it with three *A*'s: A-Aaanthony. That'd give you four *A*'s in a row, and I don't think anyone could top that."

"Aaa . . . aaa . . . aaanthony?" He repeated the name slowly, dragging out the first syllable of his name. "A-Aaanthony. Yeah. I like the sound of that. Wait'll I tell Dom he was all wrong about you."

"Wrong about me?"

"Yeah. He said you liked working with small businessmen, but that you probably wouldn't have time to help me out."

Domenic had remembered, which sent a little thrill coursing through her. But he'd made her sound so cold to Tony, which brought her right back to earth. "I'm never too busy to help a friend," she said lightly, though she knew in her heart that a few days earlier she'd have considered the effort a waste of time. Especially since she hadn't come up with anything impressive.

But at the moment Tony seemed well pleased—and well prepared. He whipped a black Magic Marker out of his pocket and hunkered down in front of the sign. He laboriously inked in his new company name, and then leaned back on his heels to admire it. "Any other ideas?

Probably not much more I can do, considering the space factor."

This was kind of fun. She crouched down next to him.

"Well, the next time you make a sign, you might want to consider using a different phrase than 'official hauler.' That sort of makes it sound like you're carrying sides of beef in the backseat."

"What can I say, it came natural on account of I used to be a teamster, but you got a point there. Dom was right, you are real smart."

"Domenic said I was smart?" Pure pleasure rocketed through her, sending her spirit soaring again. Of course she was smart. She knew she was smart, and so did everyone else. Still, it felt kind of nice to know that Domenic had noticed, and thought enough of her intelligence to boast of it to his cousin.

Or was it boasting? Suddenly she wasn't so sure.

"Domenic didn't happen to mention that I have a good personality, did he?" she asked suspiciously as Tony handed her into the backseat. Men who described a woman as being smart, as having a good personality, usually had no interest in the woman in question.

"Actually, he said you're kinda standoffish." Tony sent her an apologetic grin and then thunked her door closed.

"Oh, well, that's okay then. I think." Oh, God, she didn't know what she meant. Her thought processes had been totally screwed up ever since embarking on this new course of impulsivity. She didn't think being called standoffish was a step in the right direction. She crossed her arms and glowered at the back of Tony's seat.

"I'll tell him he was wrong about that too," Tony said.

Lynne felt the oddest tickle in her throat.

Tony clapped the helmet back on his head and settled himself in to drive. The limo moved smoothly away from the curb. No window separated the driver's compartment from the backseat; she didn't know whether it was missing, or whether Tony just hadn't bothered raising it.

"Mind keeping an eye on the sideview mirror and let me know if I cut too close?" he called. "This helmet ain't the greatest for my whatchamacallit, peripheral vision."

Lynne gulped. "Maybe you shouldn't wear it, then."

"Huh?"

"Take off the helmet."

"Huh?"

"*Take off the helmet!!*"

"What're you sayin'?"

She finally realized, from the decibel level of Tony's bellowing, and from the way the limo swerved as he craned his neck, trying to make out what she said, that the helmet wasn't the greatest for his hearing, either. And wait until she got hold of Domenic—being an ex-teamster truck driver wasn't much of a testament to one's safe-driving ability. "Keep your eyes on the road. I'll watch! You drive!" she shrieked.

"We got plenty of time. It's only about ten minutes to Dom's. He's right over in Shadyside. Say, I heard you two on the radio Friday. Sounded good together."

"We weren't together."

"Huh?"

"*We weren't together in the studio!*" Lynne paused to give her vocal chords a rest, remembering the radio interview set up by Marvin Kane. The solitary intimacy of sitting there at her desk, cradling the phone to her ear, and knowing nobody could see her, had emboldened her into laughter and joking. And Domenic had stepped in with just the right words to deflect the talk-show host when his questions skirted too close to the truth about their non-relationship. "The radio station called me at my office, and Dom in his office, and patched us up."

"Hey, it might be nice, if you could patch it up. I saw you on the noon news yesterday. Looked like you could make a nice couple. Too bad there's nothing going on between you two." Tony let go of the steering wheel to make a hard gesture, one that Lynne had always considered vulgar, to another motorist. No wonder his limo business was languishing, she thought as she gripped the armrest for balance while the limo careened toward the next lane.

Her throat ached from screaming to be heard through Tony's football helmet, but it tightened with an ache of another sort when she realized that virtually her entire relationship with hands-on Domenic had been conducted in a decidedly hands-off manner. Never calling each other, no time wasted on dating, being patched together through the miracles of modern technology. A few days earlier she would have considered this to be the perfect romantic relationship. But perfection shouldn't leave a woman cold and lonely, craving the touch of roughened fingers and trying so very hard to smile in the dark.

She pushed that thought away. "We weren't together on television, either. The camera crew came to my office on Friday. I don't know where or when they filmed Domenic. Somehow they made it seem like the reporter was talking to both of us at the same time."

"That's right, you're not the same kind of girl Dom usually dates."

"I'm not?"

Well, she'd known that, but hearing Tony say it out loud—bellow it, rather—iced over the excited little flicker that burned in her heart.

"No shortage of ladies, if you get my drift, but he usually goes for the shy type, little and round with lots of curly dark hair. Terry lasted the longest. She was a clerk at the flower shop, which gave them plants in common. Then there was Becky—she was a receptionist at Stephen's Hair Graphics—never saw fingernails like that girl's. Other than that, Dom's big on waitresses. I figure it's the food angle that draws him."

"The food angle." The iciness crusted even more as Lynne thought of her yogurt lunches, the unused oven in her condo stove. Her silk flower arrangements and neatly trimmed fingernails.

"Hey, how's that right lane?"

Lynne glanced to the side and saw with relief that the lane was clear. "Go."

Tony slid the car into the right lane. "We'll be turning just ahead. I figure I saved about three-point-two miles by picking you up first. A businessman got to cut corners every chance he gets, right? Well, here we are. Hope Dom ain't off in the greenhouse, or I'll have to sit out here honking for about ten minutes. Maybe I'll take this helmet off for a couple minutes, seeing as there ain't nobody around likely to get sucked in by my advertising campaign just now. Pretty damn uncomfortable, excuse my French, although I could get used to it if they paid me a couple mil to wear it while I knocked a few guys around."

Tony pulled up in front of an impressive Victorian mansion. The edge of a greenhouse jutted from behind the house. "I can go knock on the greenhouse door," she offered.

"Nah, Dom wouldn't like that. He never lets anyone see that goofy stuff he's growing in there."

"Not marijuana?" Lynne asked, though she didn't care what he grew, if keeping it secret meant banning well-manicured, curvy, brunette waitresses from his house.

"I should be so lucky. Uh, Lynne, that's just a joke, okay?" Tony laughed nervously. "Domenic goes in for all kinds of weird stuff—legal, but weird. Me, I like a nice flower that'll hold up good for a week or two in a vase, so you get your money's worth. Something perky, with a good smell, you know? Dom, he grows this stuff doesn't make flowers, or blooms at midnight, or lets off some god-awful stink. All plants that ain't supposed to grow in Pittsburgh, on account of he likes the challenge."

"There's not much of a challenge in growing plants in a greenhouse," she muttered, knowing Tony couldn't hear her. Didn't that sound just like Domenic Corso—calling it a challenge to raise weird plants within the walls of a greenhouse. He was a great one for nurturing, providing he could stuff the things he nurtured into the proper environment. If he didn't think something would thrive, well, he just wouldn't attempt it. Her, for example. He assumed she couldn't fit into his world. He wouldn't even risk giving her a chance.

She suddenly realized that she very much wanted that chance.

People weren't like plants, couldn't be locked away in some climate-controlled shelter protected from the forces that threatened to tear them apart. And yet people tried all the time, counting on love to strengthen them, love to protect them from those outside pressures.

Love? Where on earth had that thought come from? She didn't love Domenic Corso. She couldn't love him. She barely knew him.

Or did she?

Her heartbeat tapped out a painful awareness. Since meeting him, she'd changed. He'd encouraged her to push and keep pushing for what she wanted. He'd helped her remember to smile. He made her laugh and sent her nerves tingling just hearing his voice over the telephone. But that tingle was nothing compared to the sweeping rush that surged through her, remembering his kiss, that brief, intimate touch that hinted at so much more.

"We're in luck—here he comes," Tony said.

There was a flash of light from the beveled glass of the massive oak front door as it swung open and caught the sunlight, and then Domenic Corso came bounding down the walk.

He looked gorgeous.

She hadn't seen him for two days. At least, she hadn't seen him in person, and she refused to acknowledge the number of times she'd replayed their video kiss. She was shocked to feel the iciness melt away from her heart as he walked toward her with a huge, blindingly bright let's-go-Steelers smile. She loved the way his long legs moved in his jeans, the way his unzipped bomber jacket gaped open to reveal a well-stretched Steelers sweatshirt. She'd have to modify that one item on her specification list—her real fiancé ought to look good in casual clothes as well as a suit.

Tony pressed a button and the passenger side front window whined down. "Get your butt in gear, Dom."

Domenic slapped the limo's roof with a firm thump. "Car looks great, Tone." He opened the door and swung himself inside, bringing fresh air and glittering sunshine with him. The limo, which had seemed cavernous, suddenly felt just the right size. He sprawled next to her with the easy way men had of claiming a good bit more than their share of space. But even though he appeared nonchalant, an invisible energy seemed to vibrate from him, calling her to move closer rather than place more distance between them as was her usual inclination.

"Hi." He slanted her a grin that held more than a hint of supressed excitement.

"Hi."

"I'm really up for this game."

"Me too."

"And I'm gonna get you there in style," vowed Tony. He shifted gears, and the limo screeched off toward the city.

She was dressed for bouncing, Domenic just knew it, but he'd probably be denied the thrill of seeing it. Her down-filled jacket concealed her upper torso and the slim curve of her hips.

This was not good. He was getting off to a bad start, assessing her bounce potential when he'd sworn to treat this outing like any other trip to the ball yard with a buddy.

Except news reporters didn't chase after his car, waiting to shove microphones in his face, when he attended games with his buddies.

"I don't believe this," Lynne said, when Tony pulled up to Gate C and a horde of cameramen descended on them. "That marriage license guy is really getting his money's worth out of those tickets."

"Uh, actually, I called them." Tony shot them an apologetic grin. "I figured that since I drove you here for the publicity, well, I might as well drum some up, you know? I told them I'd drop you off here."

"Thanks a lot, cuz," Domenic ground out.

"I called them too," piped up a female voice, and Dom swiveled around to see a well-bundled brunette hurrying toward them.

"Lisa!" Lynne sounded both amazed and relieved, as if she couldn't quite believe her cousin had showed up.

"Tailgate's set up under the bridge pier."

"This was really great of you."

"Hey, what are cousins for?" Lisa grinned and gave Lynne's hand a quick squeeze. "Besides, I appreciate the opportunity, and who knows—if Domenic likes the wings, you might hire me to do your wedding."

"Oh, Lisa, I thought I told you . . ." Her voice trailed away as she took a frantic peek at the vulturish news people. She cupped her hand over Lisa's ear and whispered something that turned Lisa's eyes round with amazement.

Domenic figured he knew what Lynne said: *There's not going to be a wedding. Can't you see he's not my type at all?*

"Let's get going here, people," suggested one of the newsmen.

"Make sure you all stand in front of the sign, so people see my company name on television," Tony directed them. He jutted his jaw toward Lisa. "Did you bring a sign?"

"Sort of." She whipped a business card out of her pocket and held it against her chest. Tony grinned. So did the cameramen, and they spent a lot of time fiddling with their zoom lenses. Dom figured Lisa was in for quite a lot of attention.

Well, there was nothing to do but play along. He and Lynne faced the cameras. He wrapped his arm around her waist in a very fiancélike manner. The good thing about down jackets was that they tended to squish when pressure was applied, so she came a lot closer to him than he'd dared hope. She wore running shoes instead of the heels she wore with her business suits, and he was surprised at how nicely she tucked right below his shoulder. Lord knew what kind of goofy grin was plastered over his face; the camera people seemed pleased.

Too pleased, maybe. He caught one or two of them leering at Lynne as if imagining what they would like to do with her on the honeymoon night Dom would never have. It irked the hell out of him.

"I really hate this," Lynne said with a fake smile that he could tell she'd pasted on for the sake of the cameras. He ached to touch the edges of her lips, trace her eyelids, and remind her to smile for real. She wore a tassel cap pulled down to protect her ears against the January chill, and the breeze from the three rivers lifted the ends of her hair, whipping them against his chest. He'd never seen her with her hair set deliberately free before. He fought back the urge to wind a strand around his finger, to feel its silky suppleness curl around him.

"I hope we don't jinx the team." She bit her lip.

"Nah. We'll bring them luck," Dom said.

"Everyone expects them to lose."

"They'll do okay if they stick together and refuse to give up."

"Do you really believe that?" she whispered. "Do you really think people can overcome the odds, buck conventional wisdom, if they stick together and refuse to give up?"

"They'll never know if they don't try."

Lisa approached them with paper plates overloaded with chicken wings, nachos, and hot sausage. "C'mon, you two. You'll need your strength for cheering."

That brief snippet of conversation haunted him throughout the brief but riotous tailgate party. Lynne was a serious Steelers fan. She probably didn't mean anything by asking him what he thought about people sticking together, about fighting the odds. But what if she did? He slugged back a beer, wondering what had happened to all his resolve to hold himself aloof from her.

He swallowed the last of his beer and crushed the can. They were adults. Adults asked questions of each other, important questions, even when they weren't sure they would like the answers.

And then Lynne craned her neck. "Susan!" she cried. "We're over here. There's plenty to eat and drink."

An elegant brunette, sort of a Lynne clone, walked over with a preppie lawyer type in tow. The brunette glanced over the food, probably figuring the fat grams weren't worth it, considering that she didn't help herself to a single bite.

"Susan, this is Domenic." Lynne made the introductions. "If it wasn't for Susan, I wouldn't be here today."

"You wouldn't?" he asked.

"She's the one who shook me up, challenged me to impress her."

Susan gave her a friendly punch on the shoulder, and the two giggled like Girl Scouts celebrating their first sale of a case of cookies. Lynne, giggling. The sun glinted off her hair, and the frigid air reddened the tip of her nose, the crest of her cheeks. No business face today—she was nonstop smiles, trilling laughter that reached into his soul and twisted it with the knowledge that she'd never been so carefree with him.

She'd turned all smiles the minute her boss showed up. This meeting between Lynne and Susan smacked of a setup. Lynne's comments about bucking the odds suddenly took on a whole new meaning. She wanted to impress her boss. She wanted to be promoted. She'd told him so from the very beginning.

Well, thank God he'd opted out of corporate America. He didn't understand how a woman could savor breaking through the glass ceiling when it meant breaking some poor guy's heart.

And she was, he realized with a start. Lynne Stanford was breaking his heart. He wanted her, but she didn't want him.

He helped himself to another beer.

Later, when they were in the stands, the whole stadium felt charged with an electric energy—or maybe it was just the beers, Dom couldn't be sure. He fervently hoped his VCR had kicked on as programmed so he could see some of the game when he got home.

He didn't see much at all of the Steelers' gritty performance, even though he was there in person.

He'd been too busy watching Lynne.

She'd followed every play, nudged him in the side

when she caught some of the players pulling fakes, cursed the referees with the passion of a longshoreman. If he'd known it was this much fun going to a football game with a woman, he'd have started doing it years ago. "You're really into this," he marveled.

"I've missed this so much. Oh, Domenic, just look how nice!" She held her beer between both hands while staring mistily down at the field, where a half-dozen three-hundred-pound defensive linemen lay sprawled like beached whales in the wake of a Steelers' running back. "I can't believe I let myself forget that it's my one."

"Your one what?"

"My one guilty pleasure. The one stupid, pointless thing I allow myself to enjoy. Everybody has one."

"I don't."

She sniffed disbelievingly. "I know about your greenhouse."

"Hey, my greenhouse isn't stupid and pointless."

"Anybody can grow plants in a greenhouse. *I* could grow plants in a greenhouse. If you really wanted to challenge yourself, you'd try growing that stuff on a windowsill or something."

"Can't be done," he bit off the words.

"Did you ever try?"

"It would be stupid to try. A waste of time."

"Domenic Corso, you're a big fat faker," she said. "Lecturing me on how to take risks, when all you do is play it safe."

The insult lacked the sting of her best hedgehog efforts, but it struck a bull's-eye even so. He lost his opportunity to insult her back when the crowd roared. The Steelers had gained another first down, bringing them to midfield.

He cheered. He whistled. Along with everyone else, he stomped his feet against the steel decking until the metallic echo boomed through the stadium. He twirled his Terrible Towel until his wrist ached. But all the while it bugged him that Lynne didn't understand about his greenhouse.

Funny. He'd never expected anyone to understand, which was why he seldom talked about his hobby with anyone. He'd thought it might be different with her. She, of all people, ought to understand the quiet thrill that came from accomplishing something that everyone said couldn't be done. Instead, little Miss Brand-New-Risk-Taker accused him of playing it safe.

She's right, he thought.

The Steelers earned another first down. He watched them march methodically toward the goal while his mind taunted him with an endless procession of the women he'd marched through his life. Nice women. Safe women. Women who fit his preconceived notion of what he thought would fit best into his family, women who would always put his wishes ahead of their own, women who played it very, very safe in their own way. Not a one among them would trick him into thinking she was somebody else and buffalo an entire city into believing they were lovers. Not a one among them could send him soaring one minute and plunge him to the depths of frustrated despair the next.

Lynne was nothing like the kind of woman he'd always expected to marry. But then, apparently the kind of woman he'd always expected to marry wasn't the right kind, either, considering the bare state of his left ring finger.

Well, maybe he ought to take on a new challenge.

Maybe he ought to make *Lynne Stanford* his next project. Rip her out of her career-insulated cocoon and teach her how unsafe, how dangerous he could be. Show her the error of her ways. All he had to do was figure out some way to keep her from retreating behind her business face and freezing him out of her life once this game ended.

The Steelers scored. She jumped to her feet. She tore off her cap and tossed it high. She hopped up and down, spinning in a tiny circle, clapping and crowing with glee, while her hair swirled around her in a golden blond cloud.

She bounced. Oh, brother, did she bounce.

Yeah. Good deed. Who was he trying to kid?

He had it bad.

ELEVEN

Cheering their underdog team on to victory had been utterly exhausting, utterly thrilling, utterly satisfying.

In fact, Lynne thought, the only thing that exceeded that satisfaction was sitting alongside Domenic while the rest of the hoarse, beer-stained crowd staggered out of the stadium. A news reporter had sent a message asking them to hang around for a few minutes after the game, so they could get a picture of her and Domenic holding hands with the Steelers' winning score lighting up the scoreboard behind them.

Domenic slouched back in his seat, his long legs bent over the back of the seat in the row just below them. The pale winter sun had nearly set, and with the dispersement of the crowd, river-chilled air seeped through the stadium and settled around them. But Domenic wore his jacket unzipped as usual. And Lynne didn't feel cold at all, with their shoulders bumping up comfortably against each other. She could sit there with him that way all night, she thought, and gave her watch a quick check to see how long she might be able to drag it out before they had to leave. Before Tony drove him out of her life forever.

"It won't be long," Domenic said. "They'll be here any minute."

"Oh, that's not why I—" she began, feeling the need to explain to him that she wasn't begrudging the time she spent in his company. But just then, with the clatter of equipment and the whirring of camera motors that was becoming so familiar to her, the news crew arrived.

"Okay, we're going to need to move you around a little to line you up in front of the scoreboard," the fussy male producer ordered. "Up, up, up."

Once they rose to their feet, he poked and prodded them until they stood close to each other. "Not romantic enough," he decreed. "Put your arm around her."

"Anything to oblige," Domenic said. He pulled Lynne close.

She ignored the little thrill that surged through her at the way his arm cradled her, the way his hand cupped her elbow.

"This is not the time to be shy," scolded the producer. "We need you to get in tight so more of the scoreboard shows." Lynne tentatively wrapped one of her arms around Domenic's waist. "Both of them," the producer ordered. "Loop your arms around his waist." She had to turn sideways to comply, which brought her breasts up against the hardness of his chest. Her forearm rested against his belly in front, against the firm swell of his backside in the rear. She twined her fists together, resting them at his hip, just at his belt. Standing that way, she could feel his heartbeat thundering against her ear, which sort of surprised her, considering that her own was drumming so loud that even if all those fans came back and started pounding their feet against the steel decking, they wouldn't overpower it.

"Look up at him," instructed the producer. "And you, look down at her. Think happy thoughts. You're young, you're in love, and you helped cheer your team on to victory. Make our viewers jealous."

Lynne looked up. Domenic looked down. She could see the faint bearded shadow underlying his skin, the bemused smile curving his lips, the teasing sparkle in his eyes. *You're young*, the producer had said. *You helped cheer your team on to victory*. And he'd said something else . . . *You're in love*.

Am I? Lynne wondered.

At the moment, it was easy to feel like she was in love, standing there with Domenic holding her, with Domenic filling her arms. The late-day sun had lost its battle against the dull gray preceding twilight, but she felt bathed in a golden glow, with Domenic's warm brown eyes smiling down at her, intent and absorbed, as if nothing could possibly be more important to him at that moment than her.

Or maybe it was just the glare from the TV camera.

"Great!" the producer enthused. "Hold that pose! Monica, we're ready for you."

The camera swung away from them and focused on a brightly chattering news reporter.

"We have to stand here like *this*?" Lynne whispered.

"Mmm-hmm." Domenic's affirmative rumble vibrated from his chest into hers.

She grew conscious of his breathing, the even in-and-out of his rib cage riding up against hers. The heat of him seeped through her jacket to warm her, and his scent, a subtle, masculine blend of man and winter, carried on the breeze. Her heart started acting up again, and she tried to move away, so he wouldn't notice, but he tightened his hold on her, bringing her belly up against his hip.

"No you don't. We're under strict orders to stand this way."

"Well, you're too tall," she complained to cover her breathlessness. "I'm getting a stiff neck."

"Consider this a victory for efficiency. You won't have to do any chin lifts tonight," Domenic suggested helpfully.

His comment provoked her bittersweet laughter. She turned her face into his shirt to muffle the sound of it, and got even more disoriented with his warmth and his scent and the gloriously steady drumbeat of his heart. She could get used to this, Lynne thought. And that sounded warning bells. She wasn't having a real romance with the guy. She'd wasted hours daydreaming about him, lost precious sleep, lost her whole focus, when she should have been concentrating on ways to impress Susan into reconsidering recommending her for that promotion.

But Domenic was laughing with her, his chest vibrating beneath her cheek, his breath tickling her scalp, and she couldn't manage even one tiny regret over the way she'd spent a single minute of the past few days.

"Do you think your romance brought luck to the team?"

Lynne thought she'd imagined the question at first, and then it got repeated a little acerbically.

"*Excuse me*—do you think your romance brought luck to the team?"

"We didn't jinx them, that's for sure," said Domenic.

"That's what I want to talk to y'all about," came a deep, menacing voice from behind them.

Lynne swiveled to find a very large, very sweaty man glowering at them.

Instinctively, she shivered even closer against Domenic. But instead of growling or summoning a fierce threat, Domenic broke into a delighted smile. And he let go of her. He grabbed the intruder's hand and began pumping enthusiastically. Belatedly, Lynne recognized the man—T. J. McCord, the Steelers' premier linebacker. The two-hundred-and-fifty-pound, iron-muscled menace who that season alone had incurred three fines for employing excessive force on the playing field.

"You two been gettin' more publicity this past week than the whole team combined," T.J. said with a scowl.

"Sorry about that," Lynne offered tentatively. When he didn't lower his head and bash her back into her seat, she gained a little confidence, even though he was large, *very* large, with bulging thighs that made Domenic's well-proportioned legs look like those on a stretched-out Gumby. "We didn't mean it."

T.J. grunted.

"They just show up everywhere we go," Domenic added.

"Tell me about it." T.J. glared at the cameramen until they cringed back. "Seein' y'all plastered all over the news made us think. We wasn't s'posed to win today. We figure you might've brought us luck."

Oh, boy, Lynne thought, as she snuck a glance toward Domenic. She didn't think it would be a good idea to admit to T.J. that they really weren't romantically involved.

"You'd better be getting all this," the producer said to his cameraman. "Keep the film rolling."

"Us boys on the back line decided you'd better come to San Diego for the game next week," said T.J.

"The Super Bowl?" Domenic's jaw dropped.

"We'd never get tickets." Lynne felt obliged to protest.

T.J. rolled his eyes at her as if he suspected a deflated football had more brains. "We got a private box for you. Gimme your phone number so's my people can get in touch."

"A private box . . ." Lynne's protests died in a whisper. She whipped a business card out of her purse.

T.J. absorbed it into one huge paw. He curled his other hand into a massive fist and pointed his finger first at her, and then Domenic.

"Don't you two be doin' nothin' stupid. I don't wanna be hearin' about no lovers' quarrels before next Sunday. We got the Super Bowl at stake here. We're countin' on you."

He scowled at them until Domenic took her hand in his, and then a truly sweet, jack-o'-lantern smile lit the football player's face. "Ain't love grand," he said.

The news crew sprinted away, shouting their eagerness to get this scoop edited in time for the evening news. She and Domenic were alone in the stadium, except for the maintenance crew down on the field.

"Well, I'd heard that athletes were superstitious," Domenic said. "I didn't realize they carried it this far."

"This is awful." Lynne moaned. She shivered, suddenly cold. She'd been warm minutes before, with Domenic's arms around her. It was slowly beginning to dawn on her what had just happened. They'd been invited—ordered, actually—to go to the Super Bowl. But even worse, she'd been entertaining thoughts that she might be falling in love with a man who hadn't given any sign that he might be thinking along the same lines. "This has gotten way out of hand."

"We could always admit the truth and call this off."

"Is that what you want to do?" She held her breath, knowing that if he said *yes*, her life would return to its old dreary pattern of waiting, always waiting for something wonderful to happen and fill the empty void in her soul.

"No, I don't want to call it off," he said slowly.

Her pulse pounded, driving caution from her brain. *Tell him*, her mind urged. *Tell him you'd like to try with him. See where these feelings lead. The two of us together can overcome the odds.* The mere thought of so exposing the depth of her wanting felt like cat claws ripping away at her pride. But she would do it. If only he would give her the smallest sign, the tiniest indication that his thoughts were in accord with hers.

"I . . . I don't want to end it," she whispered. She waited breathlessly for him to notice that she'd made the most daring statement of her life.

"That's good, because in about thirty minutes, the top news station in town is going to televise a clip showing T. J. McCord telling us that the team needs us, the team wants us, the entire contingent of linebackers got together and wrangled tickets for us because they're so convinced we brought them luck."

"So you're saying that turning down T.J.'s offer wouldn't be the smart thing to do." Her throat ached with the effort of getting the words out.

"If we back out now, every football fan in the city will be convinced it's our fault if the Steelers lose."

"No other reason?" She took refuge in another Stanford success strategy: A good salesperson always pushed to make sure she knew all her quarry's objections.

"For the good of the team in general," he said. "If they're superstitious enough to think we bring them luck, then they might just flat-out give up if we don't come to the game. We have to go to San Diego for the good of the team," he said solemnly. "It's our civic duty."

"Our civic duty."

He drew back a little and looked at her warily. "Do *you* have any other reason?"

"Oh, no," she said quickly, maybe too quickly. "No. Not if you don't."

He nodded. And then he started sauntering down the steps. She liked the way he moved, lithe and graceful as an athlete. She'd have to add *move like Domenic* to her spec sheet.

That spec sheet, she suddenly realized, did nothing more than chronicle all the things she liked about Domenic Corso.

What on earth was she doing, compiling such a list of the perfect man she might find someday, when she had the genuine article standing right in front of her?

No, actually, he was getting away. Literally, in the sense that he was physically moving away from her. But also escaping her on the emotional level, because she was too frightened, too accustomed to believing she had to live up to someone else's impossible expectations. The only man who knew how to make her smile was getting away because he'd had the bad timing to show up at the wrong stage of her career.

"Domenic!" she called. "Wait!"

He stopped and peered back over his shoulder at her.

The wind ruffled his hair, sort of the way her fingers itched to do. Her mind raced as she hurried down the steps after him. She had to think of some way to keep them together over the course of the next week, some way to explore the tentative feelings inside of her. She had to push herself to take that risk—and she had to push him, too, because he was as cowardly about romance as she was, in his own way. He looked upon women as if they were the exotic plants that he nurtured in his greenhouse—fragile beings unable to survive outside the proper atmosphere, as though taking a woman like herself and asking her to become part of his big, boisterous family might make her wilt into insignificance.

But he was so darned stubborn. She could tell him and tell him until she was hoarse, and he still wouldn't believe they could be right for each other. She'd just have to trick him into making that realization for himself.

"Nobody's going to believe there's nothing going on between us if we keep this charade going," she said, a little breathlessly because she'd had to hurry in making up this plan and she wasn't sure it would work.

"So we'll explain it to them again," Domenic said.

"I have a better idea."

He cocked his chin up, inviting her to continue.

"We *show* them we're all wrong for each other."

"And how do we do that?"

"It's simple. We spend time with them. They'll see how incompatible we are. Before you know it, they'll be trying to split us up instead of pushing us together."

"I get it—have dinner with my family, stuff like that, and bicker and argue so that they know we don't get along."

The idea of arguing with Domenic roused a little ache in her chest. "Sort of."

"We never fight, Lynne."

"No, we don't. But only because we haven't had the chance." She pushed on earnestly. "We're always posing for a news camera, or trying to be on our best behavior in front of a crowd. What we need to do is tackle them in small groups, and let our natures take their course."

Oh boy, she thought, as the wind kicked up and she found herself instinctively leaning closer into him, craving his warmth. Letting her nature take its course with his might not be the smartest plan she'd ever developed.

"You don't have time for dates. Neither do I."

"Well, I'm willing to make the sacrifice. For the good of the team," Lynne said.

"That's the only reason you'll make time—for the good of the team?" He frowned at her, and she dared to hope that he was as eager as she to hear that more than a love of football might be behind her plan.

"Can you think of a better reason?" she asked with so much false innocence that she felt sure he'd see right through her.

But he didn't. And she couldn't decide whether she should feel depressed or victorious. "Okay," he said. "And I have the perfect way to begin."

"How?"

"Bowling."

"Bowling?" She'd gone bowling exactly once, and done just awful. She was about to refuse when she realized what he was up to. He expected her to decline, because he had her pegged as the kind of woman who didn't set foot in bowling alleys. "Okay, we'll go bowling."

"We will?" A little tic along his jaw told her she'd correctly assessed his motives. And then he smiled, a smirky, well-pleased sort of smile. "Bowling, tomorrow night—with your mother and father."

The notion of Madeline and Franklin Stanford tying on green-and-red-striped bowling shoes was so incomprehensible that it left Lynne speechless. But not for long, because Domenic's smirk widened with the smug satisfaction of a man who'd just won an argument.

"Okay," she said, "on one condition."

"You name it."

"Dinner the next night with your mother and your grandmother. At *my* house. With *me* doing the cooking."

"You're a bad cook?"

"I'm beyond bad. Beyond lousy. They'll be convinced you'll die of either botulism or starvation on a steady diet of my cooking." He looked crushed as any man who tended to pursue the food angle would. Well, Tony had warned her. Threatening to cook had been a dumb idea, she thought sourly, sure to send him straight into the arms of a well-manicured brunette waitress. She wasn't so great at thinking on her feet.

"Only if we invite my brothers and sisters and their spouses too," he countered. "Get them all sick at once so they won't bother us anymore."

"Deal," she said.

"Deal."

Snowflakes drifted down. One landed right on the tip of her nose while another tumbled against her cheek. "Oh, no! Tony's limo—his paint's temporary."

He thumbed the snowflakes away, and it seemed like her whole body tingled in response to that gentle touch.

He smiled down at her, his eyes crinkling, and she had the absurd notion that her concern over Tony's tiger-striped paint job had pleased him in some way.

"Let's get going, then," he said, "before our chariot melts."

TWELVE

"You did tell them we would be bowling?" Domenic asked.

"Of course I did. As you can see, *I* dressed right," Lynne added with a virtuous nod of confirmation.

She wore jeans topped by the sort of boxy bowling shirt favored by league players. Crisp creases highlighted the sleeves and shirtfront. Either Lynne Stanford was one hell of an expert with an iron, or she'd bought that shirt brand-new.

"Nice shirt," he said.

She pinkened, pleased. "I got it on my lunch hour today."

"You went shopping?"

Her rosy tint deepened into a true blush. He wanted to hug her, feeling absurdly pleased. He'd known women who seemed to own direct lines to the saleswomen at Victoria's Secret, but none of their purchases affected him half as much as knowing Lynne had gone out and bought a bowling shirt for their first real date.

Domenic glanced at her parents again. Madeline Stanford wore pure white wool slacks and a strand of pearls against her fluffy white cashmere sweater, looking as bored and glacial as Domenic remembered. Franklin Stanford must have come straight from the office. His thinning hair matched exactly the shade of his gray suit, and his crisp white shirt showed no ink stains or wrinkles.

Lynne made the introductions. Madeline remembered him with a cool smile. Franklin took his hand in a surprisingly strong grip, surprising because of the general vagueness about the man. But as they shook hands, Franklin's regard zeroed in on Domenic in a way that made Domenic believe that he wasn't as disinterested in his daughter's escapades as he seemed to be.

"You go first, Mother." Lynne settled herself into one of the seats curved around the scoring console. She poked through a big leather carryall bag while Domenic punched their names into the computer. Madeline held a bowling ball out in front of her, walked up to the line, and dropped the ball, just dropped it, without bothering to set up her shot. It rolled so slowly that it seemed to take an eternity before it caromed off the edge of the lane into the gutter.

She looked triumphant when she returned to the seat.

She'd done that on purpose, Domenic realized. She wanted to make them feel contrite for wasting her time playing this game. Well, in a way that went right along with Lynne's plan—they didn't need to roll a full game to convince her parents that he and Lynne were all wrong for each other.

But that didn't suit *his* plan.

"You know something," he mused. He'd bet anything that Lynne had inherited her penchant for efficiency from Madeline. "This would go a lot quicker if you rolled the ball instead of dropped it."

"I'll keep that in mind for my next turn."

"You get another roll. You get two chances per frame, right, Lynne?"

Lynne looked up guiltily from her carryall. "Uh, yeah." Domenic thinned his lips, all his pleasure in her bowling shirt dissipated. She'd probably stuck a time management report into that darned bag and figured to do a little work between frames.

He decided to see to it that she had plenty of time to finish her reading.

"In fact," Domenic said to Madeline. "I wouldn't mind if you took a few practice shots, just to get the rhythm of the game. You wouldn't mind, would you, Frank?"

Franklin jerked, seemingly startled that someone would call him Frank. "Not at all. Roll away, dear."

Madeline shot her husband a look laced with pure venom. He smiled back, bland and vague as can be, and then settled in his seat, staring at nothing.

This was certainly going well.

He had entered the Stanfords into the computer first, figuring it was the polite thing to do. He wished now that he'd placed himself higher in the bowling order, because maybe whaling a few sixteen-pounders down the lane would relieve some of the frustration building up inside of him.

He'd agreed to this fiasco because he'd hoped to convince Lynne that they were good together, not because of her half-baked scheme that displaying their differences in public would prove they couldn't be a couple. She was supposed to push, not pull back.

He stewed silently over her unpredictability until it was Franklin's turn. Lynne's father stood and removed his suit jacket, folding it neatly over the back of his seat. He made his approach in a very practiced manner; Domenic noticed that Madeline's mouth parted with surprise as she watched her husband's fluid movements. Franklin threw a strike. He returned to his seat, shook open his suit jacket, and put it back on.

"Very impressive, Frank," Domenic said. "Right, Lynne?"

She jumped, and pulled closed the edges of her carryall. She glanced shamefacedly toward him. "Uh, right."

"You didn't see it, did you? Your father rolled a strike."

"He did?" She blinked and stared in awe at her father. "I didn't know you could bowl, Father."

"I'm quite good, actually," Franklin said without a trace of braggadocio.

"You never bowl," said Madeline.

"Oh, but I do. All those business trips. There's always a bowling alley a short cab drive from the hotels."

Madeline sat back in openmouthed amazement.

"You're up," Domenic said gently to Lynne.

She took another wild-eyed peek into her carryall bag, and then dragged herself over to the ball carousel. She hoisted her ball, swallowed bravely, and then made her approach. But she started off on the wrong foot, so that when she let go of the ball, she hit her leg. Which made her hop, wincing in pain. Which made her bounce, and seriously put a crimp into his plan to nonchalantly ease himself over to Lynne's seat for a little covert snooping.

But a man had to do what a man had to do.

Much as he preferred watching her, he had to know what she'd hidden in that carryall that was so much more important than paying attention to the all-American pastime of bowling. He hooked a finger into the zippered opening and very casually tugged it open a little wider. He slanted a sideways glance, and all of a sudden his chest ached with a strange, bittersweet pain.

She had a bowling manual in there. It was open to a page showing how to approach the pins and where to lay down the ball. She'd highlighted in yellow the proper footsteps and the path the ball ought to take. While he'd been fuming, convinced she was sneakily trying to work, she'd been reading a book to teach herself how to bowl.

That made no sense. If her goal was to convince her parents that she and Domenic were all wrong for each other, then she'd have been better off to come to the lanes with a complete ignorance of the game, treat it with contempt the way Madeline was doing. Instead, she'd gone out and found a bowling instruction manual.

She hadn't pulled back from the challenge at all. But she was pushing with a tentative fright that told him this was one challenge that hit her where she knew she could be hurt.

Domenic felt breathless, as though he'd been poleaxed. His mind conjured the image of Lynne slinking toward him, dressed in nothing but her bowling shirt, beckoning him toward her with her highlighted bowling manual. Heat blazed through him just thinking about that starched cotton skimming the tops of her thighs and her golden brown hair tumbling down over the little name embroidered over her pocket. He muffled a groan. His fantasies had definitely veered off their usual course.

Watching her in person did nothing to relieve the heavy wanting that pounded through him. She was a fast learner. She made her second approach with more confidence. In fact, she put a cute little hop in her step when she let go of the ball, and sort of slid to one side with her head bent so that her hair swung down over her shoulders and swirled back into place. Very nice, even if the ball did curve into the gutter.

"She twisted her wrist when she threw the ball," Franklin said. "Somebody ought to go up there and give her a few pointers."

Domenic jumped up, ready to comply, and then remembered he was supposed to be helping her convince her parents that they didn't get along. Some courtship this was turning out to be, trying to win a lady's love by pretending not to care.

"You do it," he said, wondering belatedly why Franklin hadn't simply gone up there to help his daughter.

"Go on, *you* help her," Franklin said softly. He looked at Domenic with a mute pleading in his eyes that told Domenic he might want to do it himself, but wasn't sure of his reception.

None of these Stanfords seemed to be able to reach out and grab what they wanted. "I'll tell you what," said Dom. "I'll help Lynne, providing you help your wife."

Madeline didn't say no.

And so Dom touched Lynne's elbow as she backed away from the lane. "C'mon," he murmured in her ear. "I'll give you a few pointers. You're pathetic."

She bristled, just as he knew she would. Her eyes narrowed and developed steely little glints, telling him she meant to prove him wrong. Now, if he could just goad her into going after *him* with the same intention . . .

"Let's get this over with." He sighed for effect. He tried showing her by posing and pretending to roll the ball, but for a smart woman, she seemed to be having a lot of trouble understanding such a simple concept. He studied her with deep suspicion. "Are you sure you're trying?"

"I'm not very coordinated." She brushed her hair out of her eyes with a graceful gesture that made his middle clench. "I guess you'll just have to show me the way they do in the movies," she said.

"What do you mean?"

"You stand behind me and I'll rest my arm against yours—like this." She snuggled her rear end against his pelvis and pressed herself all along his front. He grabbed on to her shoulders.

"Don't move," he said, or tried to say—he wasn't sure that the strained, garbled sounds coming from his throat could be deciphered. But if she moved away, everyone in the place—including her parents—would be wondering if he'd shoved a bowling pin down the front of his pants.

"Okay." She twitched her bottom, nestling herself a little closer. "Show me that arm swing again."

He bent his arm at the elbow. Hers fit lightly, trustingly inside the angle of his. He swung back, and she moved with him, creating a sweet friction. Her hair brushed against his chin. With each breath he drew in her fresh, clean scent.

"Rats," she said.

"Huh?"

"I don't think this is working. They're not paying any

attention to us. They . . . they look like they're having fun." Lynne said in amazement.

Franklin had removed his jacket once more and loosened his tie, as well as the top button of his white shirt. He was looking downright dashing. Madeline had a few black smudges marring her right hip, where Franklin's hand rested occasionally. And the rusty, brittle tinkle that made Lynne jump turned out to be a burst of laughter from Madeline.

"Bowling's fun," Dom managed to say.

"But they never have fun together."

"They're married, Lynne. They have to have fun once in a while."

"You don't get married to have fun. A stable marriage provides each partner with baseline comforts, leaving the partners free to devote more energy to their careers." She spoke with the precision of a robot repeating lines that had been programmed into its memory.

Domenic's arousal deserted him, defeated by the horror of what she believed. He had to step away from her before he acted on the impulse to lift her into his arms and kidnap her, steal her away, far, far away, where he could prove to her that baseline comforts—whatever the hell they were—had nothing to do with marriage between a man and a woman who loved each other.

"We'll have to do this again someday," Franklin said later when they were changing back into street shoes.

"I'd like that, Father," Lynne said quietly. "Of course, Domenic won't be joining us anymore. You've probably noticed that there's nothing going on between us."

"A pity," Franklin said mildly. "I would have enjoyed matching my skill against his sometime when he didn't deliberately miss picking up his easy spares."

There was definitely more to Franklin than met the eye. Domenic inclined his head in subtle appreciation even as anger raced through him. How could Franklin have let his daughter grow up so afraid to let herself fall in love? "Will that bowling date take the place of your quarterly lunches?" he demanded.

"I'd prefer evenings, Lynne, unless your schedule won't allow."

"I can find time, Father," she whispered.

"So can I," Madeline said.

The Stanfords left, and Lynne stared wistfully after them.

"Well," said Domenic with plenty of false cheerfulness. Hearing her tell her father that he wouldn't be part of their future family bowl-a-ramas raised a warning flag that ripped through his confidence as if its edges had been soaked in acid. "How do you think that went?"

"Unbelievably well," Lynne said with a distance that made it sound as though she'd already retreated behind her barrier. If not for that manual and bowling shirt, if not for that extra little twitch of her delectable bottom, he'd be inclined to think she had no interest in him at all. But she had twitched. And she'd shopped. He was pinning a lot of hope on that bowling shirt.

"About dinner tomorrow night," Dom said.

"Yes?"

"My mother said she'll bring dessert."

Domenic's grandmother sniffed suspiciously at the foil pans of lasagna set out on Lynne's buffet. "Did you make this yourself?"

"No," Lynne said. She summoned a deep breath. "It's frozen."

Frozen. She could hear the appalled murmur sweeping through the crowd of Corsos and with a sinking heart realized that Lisa had been right—serving frozen lasagna to Domenic's family was almost as bad as offering them spaghetti topped with sauce from a jar.

But that had been part of her plan, to offer food so outrageously inappropriate that Domenic's family would decree they were all wrong for each other and try to march him right out the door. And then, if her goofy plan worked, her overly protective man would dig in his heels, order them all to eat the lasagna, and tell them that he preferred frozen over homemade, any day.

Except Domenic wasn't saying anything.

"Give me a fork," ordered Grandmama.

Everyone watched with bated breath while she sampled the lasagna. She frowned. "Show me the package," she said. Lynne hurried to the wastebasket and dug one out of the trash. Grandmama held the box at arm's length and glared at the photo of the sweet, old gray-haired lady pictured on the corner of the box.

"Thief!" Grandmama decreed, pointing a finger that shook with outrage. "She stole my lasagna recipe!"

"Not this again," muttered one of Domenic's brothers.

"Here." She shoved the box back into Lynne's hands. "Read the ingredients. Out loud, so everybody hears."

"Uh, sure." Lynne swallowed. "Enriched egg noodles, tomatoes—"

"See," said Grandmama. "My recipe."

"Everybody uses noodles and tomatoes, Grandmama," said Domenic.

"Since when did you become an expert on making lasagna?" she countered. She lifted her chin at Lynne. "Read."

"Garlic, basil, oregano, olive oil—"

"*My* recipe. She's a little off on the oregano, though."

Domenic threw up his hands in defeat. "Okay, it's your recipe. What do you think she should do, Lynne—sue the frozen-food industry?"

She knew what he expected of her. They were supposed to be convincing everyone that they didn't get along. He'd handed her the perfect opportunity for her to say something flippant, tell the Corso family that she thought their grandmother was nuts and that they were all wasting her time. Her pride roiled in protest. She was getting just a little tired of doing what people expected her to do.

"I think she ought to write a cookbook," Lynne said. "Then that way she'll earn a little money and make sure that the people who steal her recipes get the Parmesan and oregano right."

"Your girlfriend, she's a smart girl, Domenic," Grandmama said, smiling smugly.

"She's not my girlfriend."

He'd be great at local theater, Lynne thought. He never forgot his lines or deviated from his script.

"He's not my boyfriend." She backed him up, and hoped nobody noticed how halfhearted she was about it.

"I'll help with the cookbook, Grandmama," offered one of Domenic's sisters-in-law. She came up and tucked her hand around the grandmother's elbow. "If Chris will *let* me, that is."

Domenic's mother motioned to capture Lynne's attention and then shouted, "Phyllis wants to get a job. Chris is not so happy about it."

"I heard that, Ma," Chris said. "What do you think, Dom—my wife doesn't have enough to do taking care of me and the kids and the house? She wants to go back to work."

"Salad, anyone?" Lynne asked with a desperate little lilt as she lifted cellophane bags of premixed salads in each hand. Maybe she'd gone a little too far in not at least opening the.bags and dumping the salad into bowls. She'd give anything to divert their attention toward food rather than waiting so expectantly for Domenic to respond to Chris's question. She knew what he would say—that a Corso woman belonged with the kids and in the kitchen, which was incidentally why he and Lynne were so incompatible.

"Hey, Phyllis had a good job before the kids came along. They're older now, Chris, and don't need her as much."

"You always said you'd never let any wife of yours work."

"No, *you* always said that. I've never had a wife, but if I did, and it made her happy to work, then that would be all right with me."

"Oh, thanks, Dom," Phyllis said sincerely.

"Yeah, thanks, Dom," Chris added sarcastically.

Thanks, Dom, Lynne thought, wondering why it felt so absurdly good to hear Domenic come to Phyllis's defense. Why hadn't he ever explained how he felt to her? Maybe because she hadn't asked. She'd been too certain she knew how his mind worked. She didn't realize she'd been standing there holding the salad bags at her sides as if they were air traffic control flags until someone ripped them out of her hands.

And then the Corsos attacked the food.

Eventually, only a few shreds of lettuce remained in the bags, a few dribbles of dressing in the bottom of the bottles, a few crumbs of cheese and one small corner of baked-on noodles in the lasagna pans. "Okay, now for the cake," decreed Maria Corso.

She unveiled the huge tray she'd brought. *Congratulations Domenic and Lynne* said the gold lettering piped onto the dark chocolate frosting.

"Congratulations?" Lynne asked, her throat tightening.

"My Domenic is the first in the family to make it all the way to the Super Bowl," Maria said proudly.

"He could not have done it without a good woman behind him," added Grandmama.

"Too bad they're not going to stay together," said Phyllis.

"Maybe they will," suggested Cathy.

"Not a chance," said Chris. "Domenic never invited her to his greenhouse. When he takes a woman there, we'll know he's in love."

Domenic sent Chris a chilling stare.

"Oh, they can't stay together." Maria concentrated on slicing the cake into huge slabs. "They obviously have nothing in common."

Domenic lifted a brow. Lynne pretended to smile while reality bit her with the sting of a wasp. Domenic's family idolized him. She just knew there'd been a dozen cakes preceding this one, acknowledging his good report cards, his graduation from college, the launching of his business. Corsos celebrated accomplishment, no matter how small, and she had no accomplishments, not even small ones, to stack up. The family probably couldn't wait until the Super Bowl was over and Domenic went back to his florists and waitresses.

And Domenic hadn't once, not even once, responded to her bait all day.

Her plan had failed.

Domenic stayed to help her clean up, because she was looking really frazzled by the time the last crumb of cake had been demolished. He had to give her a lot of credit for taking on the whole family at one time, and she'd done him proud, but she hadn't done anything to dispel the notion that they wouldn't be staying together after the Super Bowl game.

She hadn't said a thing to contradict his mother's carefully rehearsed line, and he'd had one hell of a time convincing Maria Corso that she should say it. Even Chris's taunt about the greenhouse, which had cost Domenic twenty bucks to set up, hadn't gotten a rise out of Lynne.

His plan had failed. Only a masochistic idiot would keep trying to push her.

"Well, I guess I'll be going," he said when she closed the dishwasher on the final load.

"Coffee?" she asked.

It sounded like the polite offer made to reward the grunt who'd stayed around to help put a place back in order. "Is that all you're willing to offer?" he asked, suddenly in a savage temper.

She backed away from his fury, but not before he caught a hint of confusion quickly masked by calm. "I'd like coffee, Domenic. Besides, it's what hostesses are expected to offer."

"Don't you ever get tired of doing what people expect you to do?" She flinched. "Don't you ever think about doing something just to please yourself?"

She sort of froze in place, staring out the window above her sink even though he knew it did nothing more than reflect the interior of the kitchen back at her. "Does this tirade mean you don't want coffee?"

Exhaustion swept through him, leaving only the giddy, unsteady awareness that he'd failed. Mr. Fix-It had pushed and pulled, poked and prodded, to no avail. She wanted him, he knew she did, but on some cool, unemotional level. Not enough to break through that shell of icy resolve that had sustained her for so long. He could understand her reluctance to shatter it, because in doing so she would have to admit she'd been living only half a life.

But maybe half a life suited her. He couldn't fix that for her, not if she was content with it. She had to recognize her needs within herself and summon the strength to reach out. He couldn't do it by himself.

"I'll pass on the coffee. Actually, I'm kind of anxious to get going. My selenicereus might bloom tonight. I don't want to miss it."

"That's one of the special plants in your greenhouse, right?"

He waited, even now unable to stifle the hope that she'd ask him to take her along. Too late, he realized that a guy who earned a good living with flowers should've thought to bring her a bouquet of the real thing, instead of trying to entice her with the vague promise of a plant that might or might not decide to bloom.

He ought to just get his butt out the door. Instead, he started babbling, as though telling her more than she cared to know might tempt her to come along.

"Some people call the selenicereus a moon cereus, but it's most commonly called a night-blooming cactus. They usually bloom only once a year. I've managed to coax mine into flower as many as three times."

"You must be quite good at it."

"Its scent is incredible—just imagine gardenias, and multiply it by a hundred. Once you smell the cereus, you never forget it."

"That sounds quite lovely."

He couldn't think of any more hints to throw. He couldn't think of any more reasons to keep throwing them.

"I guess I'll be going, then." It came out sounding kind of gruff, probably because he really wanted to say something like ***ask me to stay***. Or even better, he wanted her to push back, to demand he take her with him.

"Good-bye, Domenic."

"Good-bye, Lynne."

THIRTEEN

"This is stupid," Lynne said out loud to herself for perhaps the dozenth time since she'd started driving to Domenic's house.

Stupid, stupid, stupid to go chasing after a man who'd had every opportunity in the world to invite her to come and see his greenhouse. But he hadn't—he'd only challenged her to reach out and grab what she really wanted. And now here she was, driving to his house with every intention of pounding on his beveled glass door until he let her in to smell his dumb flower, his seleni-whatever.

He was waiting with the door propped open.

He must have seen her pull into his driveway, and he watched her fiddle with her purse and her hair until she'd summoned the nerve to walk up onto the porch. Him standing there with the door open was a good sign; him standing there with his arms crossed over his chest, with a frown furrowing his brow as he watched her approach, wasn't as promising.

She could feel waves of heat pouring from the doorway, and she wasn't sure if it was his furnace working overtime or just plain Domenic. "Can I see it?" she whispered.

"See what?"

"Your thing."

His eyes widened, and his lips parted, and she mentally groaned. Of all the stupid things to say! "Your moon cereus. The night-blooming cactus."

"That's my line. Men are supposed to be the ones who invite women over to see their etchings and whatnot."

His comment struck her like a hammer blow. She'd used all her reserves of confidence to haul herself over there. She felt suddenly tired, tired of battling. Maybe it was time to give up.

"You're right," she said. "I'm sorry I bothered you."

She swung around and made her way blindly for her car.

"Lynne, wait!"

His hand caught her shoulder and stopped her unsteady progress, and he spun her gently around until she was standing within the shelter of his big body, out of the winter wind and in the warmth that always surrounded Domenic. "C'mon inside," he said huskily. "It's freezing out here."

Big mistake, Lynne thought to herself as Domenic guided her through the front door. He stood aside, letting her pass first. She felt him step into the hallway behind her and then close the two of them in his house together, with the rest of the world outside.

Big mistake.

"This is beautiful, Domenic," she said brightly, though she barely registered the gleaming wood floors, the intricately carved architectural detail, lit softly by a small stained glass lamp.

"Thanks." He made no offer to take her on a grand tour. She felt like a person who'd just barged in on a neighbor who always encouraged impromptu visits—only to find she'd interrupted him at an extremely inconvenient moment.

"The greenhouse is back this way." He led her down the hallway and into a small utility room, and then stopped. "Well, looks like you wasted your time coming here."

"What do you mean?"

"It didn't open tonight."

"Oh. You went in to see it before I got here."

"No. I wasn't in the mood, somehow."

"How can you possibly know it hasn't bloomed? Domenic, we're in a closed room staring at a washer and dryer. We're not even in your greenhouse yet."

"Doesn't matter. I told you about its wonderful scent. When the selenicereus blooms, you can smell its perfume throughout the house."

"But you said it was scheduled—"

"Not everything performs according to schedule, Lynne, no matter how well you plan."

As if she needed another reminder that her efforts had bombed! "I want to see it anyway," she said stubbornly.

"Nagging it won't do any good." But he opened the door at the far side of the room and a tropical paradise awaited them.

Lynne stepped into the greenhouse. Its air surrounded her, warm and moist and rich with the scent of soil and vegetation. If not for the snow shower spitting against the glass, she could have believed he'd somehow transported her out of Pittsburgh.

An orderly jungle grew in pots, on benches, and hanging from hooks in the ceiling supports. She remembered Tony's remarks about the weirdness of Domenic's greenhouse garden, and had to admit he was right about some of what he'd said—there was nary a perky, recognizable flower in the bunch. But the greenery twisting about had an odd appeal, wild and vibrant.

"I don't recognize any of these plants," she said.

"Thanks." Domenic grinned for the first time in hours. She could tell he loved his garden of misfits, and she wanted to bask in the glow of his quiet pride for just a little while longer, even if it clawed at her soul, knowing none of it would ever be directed her way.

"Will you tell me what they are?"

He started pointing to one large-leaved wanderer, and then stuck his hand into his pocket instead. "Oh, they're just a bunch of plants you've never heard of."

"Domenic, I . . . I'm really interested."

"Are you?" He seemed suddenly angry, furious with her. "What's the agenda behind this, Lynne?"

"I don't have an agenda."

"Then what—you have an extra hour to kill?"

"Maybe I just wanted to see what happens if we spent a few moments alone, without a camera crew or a horde of relatives watching our every move."

"You don't want to spend time with me, Lynne."

"Since when did you become the authority?"

"You've told me loud and clear a dozen times how wrong we are for each other."

"Then why can't I think of anything besides *this*?" she whispered. And she reached up and traced his clenched jaw with her finger, and when he closed his eyes and shuddered, she rose to her tiptoes and planted a featherlight kiss at the place where her fingers had touched.

With a low moan, he caught her in his arms and kissed her.

It was technically their second kiss, but she had replayed the video of their courthouse kiss so many times that she felt she knew each nuance of his touch. She was wrong. He claimed her lips with a smoldering fire that stole her breath and sapped the strength from her limbs.

He backed her up against the greenhouse wall. She felt frigid glass at her back, torrid Domenic pressed everywhere against her in the front. She lifted her chin, baring her neck for him, and shivered with exquisite delight as his lips trailed up and over her sensitive skin. She moved, trying to get a better grip on him, and something stung the back of her hand.

"Ouch!" She stiffened from the pain, and Domenic stepped away from her. She glared up, wanting to swat to death whatever had bit her at such an inconvenient moment, and saw a trailing cactus-type plant hanging from an overhead hook. She pressed the back of her hand against her lips, sucking the blood from where a spine had pierced her skin.

Domenic's gaze settled first on her bleeding hand and then up toward the plant. A rueful smile crossed his lips. "Lynne Stanford, meet my selenicereus."

"*That's* your night-blooming cactus?"

"Yep. See the buds?" He pointed to several swollen pink pods, ribbed in darker pink. "Believe it or not, they'll be pure white when they open."

"Hell of a place to hang a cactus, Corso."

"There's no better place. Look at all the buds—there must be at least twenty. Most produce only one or two flowers."

"Well, you didn't manage to make it bloom tonight." Her hand smarted, and so did her pride, hearing him wax so enthusiastic about his stupid plant's success.

"The night's not over. But then again, maybe it won't open until tomorrow." A strange, faraway expression came over his face. "I'd better take you home now."

There he went, thinking he knew what was best, thinking she needed him to take care of her. "You don't have to take me anywhere. I drove here in my own car, and I can get home by myself."

"Okay. Go home."

She gritted her teeth, wanting to remind him that mere moments before he'd been trying to kiss her over there against the insulated glass. He was one infuriating guy, didn't know from one minute to the next what he wanted from her. Unfortunately, her body was shivering in a way that told her exactly what she wanted from him.

"I don't want to go home."

"You really should go home."

"I'm not going anywhere. I'm going to stay right here until I can smell this flower." She drew a huge, ostentatious breath. His eyes zeroed in on her chest. She filled her lungs and expelled the air quickly, hoping for a heaving-bosoms effect, and knew she'd succeeded when he swallowed.

She stepped closer and pressed against him. He circled his arms around her, and any doubt she had about taking this plunge melted beneath the warmth she found when the circle was complete, when she was enclosed within him. "I'd like to stay here, Domenic. I'd like to stay right here."

He took her to his bedroom.

He simply scooped her up into his arms and carried her through his house while she whispered "caveman" in his ear—just before tugging at his earlobe with her teeth. He kissed her then, and stumbled a little over a hallway runner rug, and they both laughed and it felt so right and so good that for a little while he was able to ignore the inner voice that warned he might be going too fast, pushing too hard.

He laid her on his bed and began peeling her clothes away. He ran out of clothes far too soon, because he knew there were a few more layers that had to be peeled off before he got to the real Lynne Stanford. Those layers weren't as easily shed. And she clung to them, maybe without realizing it, but when she pulled him down and he felt her skin so warm and soft and pliant against his, his sanity deserted him.

The hell with patience, he thought, claiming her mouth with all the frustration he'd felt over these past days. The hell with nudging her and tricking her into responding to his challenges. The hell with waiting for her to come to the realization that they could be oh-so-right. Maybe it was time to quit depending on their brains and start listening to their bodies. Lynne loved a challenge. He meant to give her as much challenge as she could handle.

His bold, proud beauty with her ever-so-straight posture and carefully set shoulders melted beneath him like the earth greeting the spring thaw. She was always so careful to maintain distance between them, but now her hands slid over the backs of his thighs, traced his hips, skimmed his waist, as if she needed to fill her hands with all the touches she had denied herself. Good God, if this was her way of accepting a challenge, he was all for it.

She thought love would wait, that she could postpone passion until the appropriate time. He wasn't letting her out of this bed until she admitted she might be the tiniest bit wrong. He wanted to wake her up to the realization that no damned lists, no two-level promotion, meant more than her woman's happiness.

The gas lamps lining his sidewalk cast a soft glow through the bedroom windows, illuminating her face, revealing her mouth parted in rapture, her eyes closed while sensation shivered through her. Her hair spread over the pillows and tumbled up against the high old Victorian headboard. She pulsed for him, she throbbed for him, and he could not deny himself the feast she presented. She made soft, throaty sounds and trembled as he trailed endless, hungry kisses all over her, everywhere.

He had his lips pressed hard against her, low on her belly, and felt the telltale ripples deep inside. He smiled against her skin. Prim, proper Lynne Stanford was one wild hellcat in bed.

"Domenic?"

She threaded her fingers into his hair, and he felt her hesitation.

"Don't worry. I have protection."

She relaxed ever so slightly, meltingly, again, and it was the hardest thing he'd ever had to do, to lift himself away from her and deal with the condom.

The condom seemed to embolden her. Or maybe it was mere curiosity—whatever, he blessed it when she used her hands and her lips and her tongue to explore and taste him from head to toe. Of all the ways he'd imagined loving her, he'd never envisioned her taking such an active role. Her natural reserve made her seem like an Ice Princess, who would never consider bestowing her favors upon some hardworking, hands-on caveman type. He gasped when her tongue circled his navel. Maybe that natural reserve of hers wasn't so natural at all. It took a warmhearted, nurturing woman to share lovemaking the way Lynne Stanford was doing it. Exactly the sort of woman his heart had been waiting to find.

She lifted her head from his belly and stared at him. The golden glow warmed her skin and kindled the hunger in her eyes.

With a low growl, he swiveled them, reveling in the feel of her long limbs twining with his and then the stroke of her toes as she wrapped first one leg and then the other around his waist. She was hot for him, and her tremors quaked through him as he slowly filled her. She gasped, and he caught her breath in his with a kiss.

Her passion rocked him, and while he lost himself in her depths, while his pulse soared in tempo with hers, some small part of him wondered how many impressions he had of her that were wrong. And how many were dead-solid right.

He loved her there on a bed that someone had built a hundred years in the past, for a lady who never dreamed of to-do lists and sales meetings and promotions. Neither did she, at that moment, at that breathless juncture where female flesh met male and they tasted and touched without being aware of how wrong they were for each other. The wonderful old bed creaked and thumped as if happy to be doing its job again. Those sounds mingled with her breathy moans and filled his head with the intoxicating tempo of love.

Lynne rocked against him. Lynne's tongue waltzed with his, and Lynne's heat coursed through his blood. Lynne's need shivered through them both, and he lost his last thread of sanity.

Sanity, he decided, was a highly overrated commodity.

She cried his name and arched against him, her skin slippery and sliding against his. Her eyes came open, and he watched them shimmer with amazement and hunger and awareness. He barely held on to his control. This was what he wanted—he wanted this glorious woman to bloom into life in his arms, to put herself first for once, to reach out with her need and satisfy his in the bargain. This could not be wrong.

Her eyes focused on his, and she called his name again, with wonder and a hint of fear that he might not be with her on this. She lay open to him, vulnerable as only someone who had never known anyone she could count on could be.

He showed her that neither of them ever had to be lonely, ever again.

FOURTEEN

Lynne tried to ease her way out of his bed, but his arm snaked out and caught her, pulling her back into the warm nest of his body.

"Stay," he said. "Spend the night."

"I can't. I didn't bring any clothes with me."

He levered himself up onto one arm and swept a slow, lazy smile over her naked form. "That's just how I like you."

"I have to go to work in the morning."

"That dress you had on tonight looked great."

"A dress? I couldn't go to work in a dress. Nobody would take me seriously." *Women executives always wear power suits*, another one of the Stanford success strategies. She scrambled out of the bed.

"Then call in sick and spend the day here, in this bed, with me," he said, flopping back down against his pillow. "I promise I'll take you . . . seriously and otherwise."

The promise in his voice, the stroke of his fingers tickling her thighs, called to her, urged her to stay.

"I can't, Domenic. In case you've forgotten, we're going to San Diego, so I'll lose the whole weekend. I've already scheduled a vacation day for Monday."

"So go in a couple of hours late."

"I can't do that either. I'm running out of time to impress Susan into recommending me for the promotion, and I promised Daniel and Beth I'd meet with them so we can work out a new approach for the Penn-Gellis account, and . . ." her explanation trailed away when she saw him stifle a huge yawn.

"I'll call in for you." He held out his arm in sweet invitation. "C'mon back to bed, Lynne."

She stood there, and the chill that settled over her didn't stem completely from her state of undress. He thought he could call off work for her, as if doing so was just one more minor task he could shoulder that would fix everything. He didn't understand. She whirled away from him and yanked her dress on over her head, not even bothering with her underwear. She groped for her shoes. She heard his low, confident chuckle and the creak of bedsprings and within a few heartbeats he was standing behind her and his arms were around her.

"Don't go," he whispered, his mouth traveling against her hair and down the side of her face to her neck. She felt the rasp of his skin and the silken wetness of his tongue as he trailed hot kisses along the curve of her shoulder up to her ear. "Don't go."

She subsided against him while waves of sensation washed over her. She closed her eyes and felt his heartbeat against hers and found herself ready to murmur in agreement. She wanted to promise to stay with him that night and for always.

"Don't go, Lynne. Stop trying to be what everyone thinks you should be. Show me the real Lynne Stanford."

Terror slammed through her. She'd been right to fear that falling in love with him would ruin everything. They'd made love one time and already he expected things of her that she didn't know how to give.

For all her life, she'd aimed at the kind of success that would earn her parents' pride. Her ambition had fostered a sense of purpose, which gave her the only security that she could cling to. Going for that corner office was all she knew how to do. Once Domenic figured that out, he'd be disappointed in her.

"I am the real Lynne Stanford. And I have to go."

He said nothing, just stepped back and stared at her, while bleakness took over his features. He didn't try to stop her when she ran through the door.

She passed blindly through the darkened hallway and down the stairs to the front door. She shrugged into her coat and was about to let herself out the door when she couldn't resist pausing long enough to run a finger over the beautiful beveled and leaded glass. Domenic surrounded himself with quiet beauty, with unexpected treasures. You never knew where you'd find it . . . like now, wishing she could disappear but anchored in place by a tantalizing hint of perfume.

That was no plug-in air freshener, and she doubted Domenic had stolen down there to spritz a heady floral essence to celebrate her departure. His selenicereus. His night-blooming cactus. It had to be. He'd been waiting all year for it to bloom, and now he was up in his bedroom and would never know. That flower meant as much to him as going to work in the morning meant to her.

But she couldn't go back to his room, she couldn't. It

wouldn't be fair to him—he'd think she was returning for another romp . . .

Who was she kidding? She couldn't go back because she would be tempted to fling herself down on that big, welcoming mattress and say *tell me again that you think the real me might be worth loving.* She couldn't do that. If she failed, she would lose everything—the promotion, her pride. Domenic.

She couldn't bear seeing his disappointment when he finally figured out there was nothing inside her worth treasuring.

But sneaking out without telling him about his flower would be wrong. She would tell him about the moon cactus and then bolt out the door before he could touch her. Good God, they were forever advancing and retreating from each other, and she didn't know what to do to keep them together. Maybe nothing could.

"Domenic," she called.

It took forever for the sound of a creaking board to announce he'd heard her. He came to the top of the stairs. He'd pulled on his jeans. She could see the pale blur of his crossed arms against the dark thatch of his chest hair.

"I think your flower opened."

He bounded down the steps with disconcerting speed. He lifted his head, sniffing the air like a hound on the trail of a rabbit. So much for her worries that he'd try to press her back into bed. The hot sting of rejection burned at the back of her throat.

"I think you're right." He grabbed her hand, not giving her the chance to refuse. "Come with me."

The scent grew stronger and stronger as they raced through the rooms, so rich and exotic that it enveloped her more with every footstep, as though she were being twirled up in yards of perfumed silk. Domenic switched on the lights in the greenhouse, and the selenicereus hung from the ceiling in all its glory, with a cascade of saucer-size, pure white blossoms seeming to pour from its heart.

"It's beautiful," she whispered, knowing the compliment was inadequate but unable to think of anything that would accurately describe the incredible flowers.

"So are you."

Her eyes filled with tears. She looked down at her feet so he wouldn't see.

"These blooms will die in a few hours," he said. "I'll stay here and enjoy them for a while."

She wouldn't sleep that night, either, especially if her mind was tortured with thoughts of Domenic all alone in his greenhouse. She peeked up at him. "Maybe . . . maybe I could stay for a few minutes too. If you wouldn't mind."

He looked at her from beneath hooded lids for a long, long moment. He was going to say no, she could just tell. She clutched her purse handle a little tighter, took a tentative step backward.

She'd asked to stay.

Domenic fought the urge to shout his triumph to the sky.

He'd been lying in his bed, listening to the sounds of her leaving him, immobilized by the sickening realization that he'd made a horrible mistake. He'd scarcely been able to believe his ears when she'd called to him.

And now she'd asked to stay, and her request hadn't come from his deliberately trying to push her away. She had reached out. Tentatively, true, but she'd reached out nonetheless. He had another chance. And he was so scared of screwing it up that he didn't know what to do. All those years of chafing under his role as Mr. Fix-It hadn't taught him a thing about what to do when something was really important to him.

Maybe a little dose of truth would be appropriate.

"It was wrong of me to ask you to call off work," he said. "You very clearly stated good reasons why you have to go, and I should have respected them."

"Really?" she whispered.

"I'm not saying that I'll never ask you again. There will be times, Lynne, when it will be okay for you to put us first."

"Us?"

He pinched one of the blooms off the night-blooming cactus and tucked it behind her ear. The heady essence of the flower mingled with the scent of his loving that still lay upon Lynne, and his body roused. He throbbed, ready and willing to prove once again how well suited they were to each other. But he knew he couldn't act on that impulse. She trembled, ready to run for cover. "After what happened upstairs, I'd say there's a definite possibility that *we* are now *us*."

"Upstairs was . . . nice."

"Just nice?" he prompted.

"Very nice?"

He watched her struggle with her response. He understood. She couldn't insist that they'd shared something extraordinary without making herself look like a fool for running away from it. He ached, wishing they could be done with these games, but the only way that could happen was for his fragile beauty to find the strength within herself to reach out and claim what she wanted. What she *needed.*

"Upstairs went way beyond nice, Lynne. There's a definite potential for terrific, and maybe extraordinary."

"Or maybe not," she said. "Maybe you'll figure out we're not suited for each other after all."

He stood there helpless to staunch the moisture brimming in her eyes. He didn't know how to fight against invisible enemies that were so insidious, so firmly entrenched, that their host didn't even realize they were slowly destroying her.

"This has all been a mistake," she whispered. "We've let ourselves get caught up in all the hoopla. We have nothing in common. I don't know how to do any of the things that are important to you."

She had that ready-to-bolt look. He'd made one mistake already, a little earlier, when he'd urged her to break through her proper and polished veneer all by herself. He couldn't even imagine how terrifying it must be for her to face that she'd been wrong all her life. But the woman he sensed simmering below those careful layers could survive. He just had to figure out a way to ease the transition for her, but she wasn't ready to let him absorb her pain. Fighters prepared for their big bouts by sparring, and he sure knew how to prod Lynne into taking jabs.

"You're right," Domenic managed to squeeze through his throat. "We could no more make a go of a relationship than, say, that orchid over there could thrive if you took it home and put it on your windowsill."

He went to the far end of the greenhouse and picked up a potted phalaenopsis orchid. The creamy white, mauve-tinted beauty seemed less lustrous when placed next to Lynne, who still bloomed with the blush from having his cheeks rasp against hers, whose lips were still swollen and reddened from his kisses.

"How can you grow cactuses and orchids in the same greenhouse?"

"I'm good at giving each the special attention it needs." He didn't bother explaining about the special fans and exhaust system he'd installed that kept one section of the greenhouse moist and humid, the other arid as a desert.

"Tony told me you used to date a girl who worked in a flower shop. I don't know why you ever broke up with her."

That tentative little hedgehog sting lifted his spirits. "*She* probably could take care of this plant," Dom said.

"I heard that snide little inflection in your voice. You don't think I can keep that orchid alive, do you?"

Hope thumped through him. He wondered if she was as aware as he of the undercurrent of their competition over the orchid. The plant was like Lynne, he thought, beautiful and deceptively fragile, but with a core of steel. Hell, these orchids were so hard to kill that they sold them in Wal-Mart. But a woman who seldom shopped—except for bowling shirts—wouldn't know that.

"Not a chance. If *you* took that orchid home tonight, it would die before we go to the Super Bowl."

"That's the trouble with you, Domenic Corso. You don't have faith in anything." Her chin lifted. "You think that things can't exist outside of some false, sheltering world that you've created for them. You think nobody can stand on her own two feet without you nearby to hold her up."

She was right, he realized. For all his life, he'd been

searching for a woman to fit into a world that existed in his own mind. In his own way he was as ruled by his upbringing as she was, limiting himself to the type of woman who he thought might blend with his family, who might match up with what his family expected of him. No wonder he'd never found anyone. Just like Lynne, he'd been trying to please everyone else instead of himself.

And he found Lynne Stanford—every stubborn, ambitious, vulnerable inch of her—eminently pleasing.

"Then prove me wrong," he challenged her.

Her chin notched higher. She held out her hands for the orchid.

"Not until we establish the stakes," he said, levering the plant to his side, out of her reach.

"Stakes?"

"Well, sure. You say you can keep the orchid alive. I say you can't. There has to be a prize for the winner."

She narrowed her eyes suspiciously, and he worried that he might have overplayed his hand. "What do you get if you win?" she asked.

"Something simple. Something easy. Something that's no skin off your nose."

She narrowed her eyes a little more. "Specify."

"You just have to admit I'm right."

"Right about what?"

"About *everything,*" he said expansively.

She sniffed. "Well, if I win—*when* I win—you have to admit that I'm right too," she said.

"About what?"

"About . . . about people being able to beat the odds, providing they're willing to fight."

"I can live with that," he said softly.

FIFTEEN

"What on earth is *that*?" Susan asked, stopping dead as she walked into Lynne's office Friday morning.

"It's an orchid."

"Really? I never saw a live one—just corsages." She went up to the plant and sniffed at the blooms. "Maybe I still haven't seen a live one. This one's pretty sad looking."

Like me, Lynne thought. "It's not doing so well."

Understatement of the year. She'd carried the plant to work with her as if staring wishfully at it for hours on end might make its leaves lift toward the sun once more, its fragile stem regain some backbone.

She'd fed it megadoses of plant food. She'd even talked to it. She'd steamed up her bathroom by running the shower and stuck the pot in the empty tub once she was convinced the atmosphere almost perfectly matched Domenic's greenhouse. Nothing had helped. The plant hadn't responded, just wilted more and more with each passing minute. Drooping, less alive, sort of like the way she'd moped around ever since leaving Domenic.

"Maybe you ought to ask Domenic for some advice," Susan suggested. "You're leaving soon for the Super Bowl, right?"

"We have a red-eye flight that'll get us into San Diego a couple of hours before the game." Lynne slumped miserably. She'd hoped to travel to the Super Bowl in a state of triumph, having convinced herself and Domenic that sheer determination could help them overcome the odds. Boy, was she ever dumb, pinning all her hopes on a stupid plant.

"Well, call him up and ask him what to do with the darned thing before it really dies."

If only she could! But he'd only be disappointed in her. She'd failed. She'd tried to succeed at something that was important to him, and all she'd done was prove she couldn't live up to her claims, the way she'd been disappointing people all her life.

"He gave that orchid to me on a dare," Lynne said. "I lost." *Big time.*

Susan wrinkled her nose sympathetically. "Well, maybe I can help you feel a little bit better. I've reconsidered my position. I'm going to recommend you for the promotion."

Lynne could only stare wordlessly at Susan.

"There's still no guarantee that you'll get the job."

"What made you change your mind? Don't tell me it was that marriage license application thing."

"That was definitely part of it," Susan admitted, to Lynne's surprise. "But more than that, it was the way you handled yourself afterward. You seemed to bring a new enthusiasm into work every day, Lynne—the way you pitched in to help Daniel and Beth with the Penn-Gellis account, for example. That showed you had the company's best interest at heart, not just your own personal agenda."

She'd made that offer because Domenic had reminded her how much she'd enjoyed selling. She'd been more enthusiastic about her job because everything about these past couple of weeks had shimmered with new excitement, as though a crystalline beacon bathed her life in new light. A light that flared from Domenic and enveloped her in its healing glow.

"Well, what do you think about that?" she murmured to the orchid once Susan left.

The orchid drooped.

She felt a sympathetic lurching in the vicinity of her heart. Odd, how Susan had just rekindled her hope for the promotion, and yet if she had a choice, Lynne would rather have the orchid alive and well and bursting with vigor so she could shove it into Domenic's arms when he met her at the airport. Oh, how she had savored the hope that he'd truly meant it when he'd said he wanted the real Lynne Stanford! True, hearing his declaration had initially sent her into a panic, but accepting the truth about herself took some getting used to. With Domenic beside her, urging her, reveling in her successes and laughing her through her mistakes, she might be able to make those changes. She'd invested every ounce of hope, every shred of longing into doing something that would convince him there was something within her worth nurturing. If only he would tell her again and again, she might dare believe him.

But she'd lost. And now she'd have to admit he was right about everything, and she knew exactly what he would make her admit: Everything in this world required the proper environment in order to thrive, and she did not belong in his world.

Domenic's pulse—none too steady—pounded off the scale when Lynne flung open her condo door. "You! I thought Tony would pick me up on the way to your house."

"I wanted to see for myself who won the bet." He strolled with deceptive casualness into her gleaming foyer. "Where's the orchid?"

"In . . . in the kitchen," she said.

He whistled tunelessly as he sauntered toward the kitchen. She followed, dragging her feet over the thick gray carpet as if it sucked at her shoes. He didn't understand. He'd expected she'd bound ahead of him, all smiles and smug satisfaction. There was no way she could have lost the bet. She couldn't have killed that orchid unless she'd taken a hatchet to its stem.

No mauve-tinted white orchids greeted him in the kitchen, though. "So, where is it?"

"Over here."

Moving as slowly as someone wading through hip-deep mud, she opened a cabinet door and pulled out a rolling trash basket. His stomach started sinking. She reached into the trash bin and came up with a flowerpot. A flowerpot holding a blackened, withered stem topped by a few brownish-green leaves that curled in on themselves as though begging to be left alone.

"You killed it!" he said in disbelief.

She nodded miserably.

"You couldn't—" he bit off his words before blurting

out that it should have been impossible to kill that orchid, at least so quickly. She'd know then that he'd set her up.

"I couldn't do it," she said. "You were right."

"Lynne—"

"I tried. I really tried. I watered it and fed it, and then watered and fed it some more, and, well, it didn't like me, I guess."

No wonder it had died. She should have just parked it on the windowsill and left it alone, and it would have done just fine. But she'd tried too hard, the way she always did. She worked and worked at gaining everyone's love and approval, when all she had to do was be herself.

"We have to talk about this," he said.

She raised a hand, imploring him to stop. "Not now, please, Domenic. Can we just put it off until after the game?"

"Uh, sure." His mind raced. Nothing was going the way he'd imagined. He needed time to regroup, to figure out what to do. No way was he going to let one dumb plant ruin his future.

Subtlety hadn't done the trick. A woman who had trouble believing in herself needed a grand gesture, something that left no doubts about how much she was treasured.

He'd think of something. He always did.

It was lack of sleep coupled with jet lag that made everything feel so weird and distorted, Lynne thought. Because of the last-minute nature of their trip, they hadn't been able to secure seats next to each other, so they flew all the way to San Diego sitting ten rows apart.

The enforced separation had seemed like a small mercy. She didn't know how she would have been able to take sitting next to Domenic for five or six hours while he rubbed it in about her losing the bet.

But maybe that wasn't fair. He hadn't mentioned the bet at all, not during the ride to the airport, not while they waited to board the plane, and not now, while they sat in the elegantly appointed luxury box, waiting for the game to begin.

She was surprised to find that nobody had joined them by the time the national anthem began. She realized then that she'd been hoping for someone else's presence to dilute the tension vibrating between herself and Domenic.

He bolted to his feet and sang lustily, with his hand pressed over his heart, right where she longed to snuggle. Where she could have been nestled right now, if she hadn't killed his orchid.

The Dallas Cowboys had won the coin toss. Using their advantages in weight, talent, and experience, they scored a quick touchdown.

"I have to leave for a few minutes," Domenic muttered.

"Fair weather fan," she shot back. "They can do it. All they have to do is stick together and fight like a team."

"I don't want to talk about teamwork just now." She flushed, remembering how she'd tried so hard to convince him that attitude was everything. "I'll be back."

With him gone, the luxury box felt stifling. The thick pile carpeting and leather sofas reminded her of home. Real walls closed in the sides and rear, while a heavy-duty pane of glass allowed her to view the crowds and the game. The noise reached through, muted and distant. Air-conditioning hummed, denying her the smell of hot dogs and nachos. She was perfectly pampered and insulated in that box, isolated from everything real. Watching but part of nothing, the way she would always be, now that Domenic had lost interest in urging her to break free.

A dreadful sensation trampled her, worse than being overrun by the entire Dallas Cowboys team. After today, she would really truly never see him again.

She wanted to burst into tears when he let himself back into the box almost at the end of the second quarter.

"Tell me something," he said, making no excuse for his lengthy absence. "Exactly when did that orchid die?"

"Saturday afternoon. A few hours before you picked me up."

"So if we had taken a plane out on Saturday *morning*, then the orchid would have still been alive, and you would have won the bet."

"Why, yes, I would have."

"Don't look so happy. You still lost."

"By a couple of hours." She sniffed. "A mere technicality. My timing was a little off."

"Timing is everything," he said.

He was right. She'd thought he'd shown up at the wrong time in her life. She'd thought she could ignore the call of her heart and send him away until her schedule allowed her to find the perfect man. She'd been a fool.

"Time for you to pay up," he said, with an anticipatory gleam in his eye. A faint roar filtered through the glass.

"Domenic—the Steelers just tied the game."

"Yeah, yeah, teamwork and all that. The first thing

you'll have to admit is that you just pay lip service to the concept."

"That's not true," she whispered.

"Oh, yes it is. If you had just called me—just once—I could have helped you keep that orchid alive. We could have done it together."

She'd wanted to do it on her own, wanted to convince him she could do something he said was impossible . . . just the way she'd spent all these years trying to prove to her parents that she could do better, fly higher, than anyone.

"All right. I admit you're right about everything."

"Not enthusiastic enough."

She clutched her hands into fists, pressed them against her heart, and fluttered her eyes at him. "Oh, Domenic, you're right about everything," she squeaked in a little-lady voice.

"A definite improvement," he said with an easy grin. "But still not good enough. I want you to repeat every one of my infallible insights after me."

She drew back warily.

"Repeat after me: Domenic Corso, you're a jerk." When she gaped at him in openmouthed astonishment, he gave her a little nudge. "Go ahead, say it."

"Domenic Corso, you're a jerk?" she repeated, but with a little question at the end, like one of those clueless Valley girls, because she couldn't understand what he was up to.

"And now say, I'm the best thing that ever happened to you, and you've been fooling around playing games instead of convincing me how rare and special I am."

The warmth that always surrounded her when she was with him reached into her and wrapped itself around her heart. "You're the best thing that ever happened to me—" she began.

"Uh-uh." He admonished her with his index finger tapping her nose. "You're supposed to say it exactly—*'I'm* the best thing that ever happened to *you.'* "

"But I'm not," she whispered. "You're wonderful and everybody looks up to you and you can do everything you promise. I failed. You can't . . . you can't ever be proud of me."

"Oh, God, Lynne." He groaned and pulled her into his arms, and she felt his heart thunder against hers. "Can't you see how terrific you are? You're bold and brave and beautiful, and that's just the *B*'s."

"What about *C*'s?" Oh, God, he was saying everything—*almost* everything—she longed to hear. She couldn't get enough.

"Courageous and curvaceous and cute."

"I thought hedgehogs weren't cute."

"I'll admit I prefer you in your uncurled state." To prove his point, he ran his hand from her neck to her waist, tracing her, toying with the hem of her Steeler's sweatshirt, and dipping his fingertip into the beltline of her jeans. She shivered against him.

"*D*'s," she whispered.

"Dedicated and determined and a dynamite kisser," he said, and swooped down over her, claiming her lips.

They'd barely gotten started when the door to the luxury box burst open and a news crew from Pittsburgh swarmed in to join them.

"Domenic," she said against his lips, "I'm really getting tired of these people."

He laughed, his breath mingling with hers before he

pulled away. "Don't be too angry with them. I asked them to come."

"You? Why?" She struggled to sit upright.

"Three minutes, Domenic," called a cameraman.

"Three minutes until what?" Lynne asked.

"Until the network picks up this feed for the halftime show and beams it into a couple of hundred million households," said Domenic.

"Are you going to make me admit to the whole world that I lost that bet?" she asked. She would do it. It seemed a small price to pay for all he had given her.

"Nope. I'm going to let the whole world watch while I ask you to marry me."

"Marry you?"

"You could say no," he suggested. There was a very mischievous twinkle in his eyes, but underlying it smoldered a depth of love that dared her to put her hand in his and shatter all their barriers. Together.

"Fat chance," she whispered over the burgeoning love that threatened to overwhelm her. "And you won't be able to change your mind afterward, because I'll have it on tape—not to mention all those hundreds of millions of witnesses."

"Okay, we're ready," interrupted the producer. "Sara has a thirty-second intro, and then you're on, Domenic." The video camera focused on the reporter, and she donned a professional smile. "Pittsburgh's Steeler Sweethearts took us all by surprise today, telling us that they'd pretended to be engaged just for the chance of winning tickets to last week's AFC Championship Game. But then their pseudoromance brought the team luck—"

"I got lucky too," interjected Domenic, and Lynne kicked him in the ankle. "Ow. What I meant is, I found the lady of my dreams. Lynne Stanford—I love you. Will you marry me?"

"I love you too," she whispered. "So, yes."

Domenic kissed her, a gentle whisper of a kiss, infinitely tender and yet ripe with the promise it would take a lifetime to explore.

Some vague, distant part of her mind knew the news crew still filmed, completing its story. The dull roar of the crowd announced that something exciting had happened on the field. But none of it mattered. Not with Domenic holding her, kissing her, loving her.

"Okay, that's a wrap."

But this kiss had not come about for the sake of a news item. It took a long, long time before they ended it, with the welcome realization that the crew had disappeared with their customary quickness. They were alone together, as they'd been before, but now everything had changed.

"Now where were we?" Domenic mused. He reached back and locked the door, and then pulled her down onto the overstuffed leather sofa with him. "I think we'll skip straight to the *N*'s, for naked."

"Domenic, the game—"

"I set my VCR."

"So did I."

"Wonderful inventions, VCR's. Now, I'd better get busy here. You have a tendency to scream when you, um, enjoy yourself, so I'll have to get the timing just right so you sort of blend in with the crowd noise."

"Domenic . . ." she gasped when he peeled her sweatshirt away, but she knew he'd just begun. He would never stop stripping the layers from her until he got to the real Lynne Stanford buried deep inside. "Don't ever change."

"Don't you change either." His breath traced over her belly, and he punctuated every word with a wet little kiss. "But, uh, Lynne—hands off my orchids, okay?"

"Okay." She delved down, found the snap of his jeans and something more interesting. "I'll just have to figure out another way to keep my hands occupied."

THE EDITORS' CORNER

Think about it. How would you react if love suddenly came up and bit you? Would you be ready to accept it into your life? Well, in the four LOVESWEPTs we have in store for you this month, each hero and heroine has to face those questions. Love takes them by surprise, and these characters, in true-to-life form, all deal with it in different fashions. We hope you enjoy reading how they handle that thing called love!

The ever-popular Fayrene Preston continues her Damaron Mark series with **THE DAMARON MARK: THE MAGIC MAN**, LOVESWEPT #878. Wyatt Damaron is sure he's dreaming. Even so, he can't resist following the lovely woman in period dress beckoning to him from the mist. As the mist recedes, Wyatt realizes that his sweet-talking sprite is flesh-and-blood contemporary Annie Logan. Wyatt is most definitely a man unlike any Annie has been used to, but something about the danger and passion lurking in his eyes has her thinking more than twice about him. He is a spellbinding sorcerer who promises to dazzle and amaze her, and in that he doesn't fail. He'd vowed to protect Annie from all that threatens to keep them apart, but will Annie trust him long enough to let him succeed? Fayrene doesn't disappoint in this sizzling novel that powerfully explores the fate of kindred spirits whose destinies are forever entwined.

Cheryln Biggs takes you on a high-speed chase through Louisiana low country in **HIDDEN TREASURE**, LOVESWEPT #879. Slade Morgan and Chelsea Reynolds are both out to recover a priceless pair of stolen antique perfume bottles—but for different reasons. For Slade it's a job he's been hired to do, for Chelsea it's a chance to prove she can accomplish more for her company in the field than behind a desk. A dangerous game of cat and mouse ensues, making for close quarters and breathless adventure. You'll be glad you came along for the ride as one reckless rebel of a hero meets his match in an unlikely damsel in distress.

Author Catherine Mulvany returns at her humorous best with her second LOVESWEPT, #880. Mallory Scott has always had trouble trusting men. Wouldn't you be **MAN SHY** if your boyfriend of eleven years left you for your own sister? Now Mallory has to find a date for the happy couple's upcoming nuptials. But he can't be just any man, he has to be one hunk of a guy. Enter Brody Hunter. Sexy mouth, silver gray eyes, tousled chocolate brown hair—in short, drop-dead gorgeous. More than enough man to ward off the pitying looks sure to be given her at the wedding. Brody can't understand why the beautiful Mallory has to hunt for an escort, but who is he to argue with good fortune? Will the potent attraction they feel be strong enough to convince Mallory to drop the carefully planned game of let's pretend? Let Catherine Mulvany show you in this outrageous romp of a romance!

Please welcome newcomer Caragh O'Brien and her stunningly sensual debut, **MASTER TOUCH,** LOVESWEPT #881. When worldly art dealer Milo Dansforth requests art restorer Therese Carroll's services, she's not sure she wants the hassle. She's quite satisfied with her quiet existence. But Milo is counting on Therese's loyalty to her father to ensure that she'll take on the job—she's the only one with the expertise to do the restoration on his priceless portrait. In a makeshift art conservatory set up in a Boston studio, Therese races the clock to finish the project and discover the secrets that lay beneath the surface of both the painting and its mysterious owner. Milo tantalizes Therese with his every touch, and suddenly the painting is not the only thing these two lovers have in common. Caragh O'Brien's talent shines bright in this tapestry of tender emotion and breath-stealing mystique. Look for more from Caragh in the near future!

Happy reading!

With warmest wishes,

Susann Brailey

Joy Abella

Susann Brailey	Joy Abella
Senior Editor	Administrative Editor